"Did you have anything at all to do with the death of my father?"

Chase blinked as if something about Maisy's bluntness surprised him. But then he looked down at her again, his gaze strong and unflinching. "No, ma'am."

"Then how did my father's cross end up in your home?"

"I have no idea."

Her gut said he was telling the truth, but her brain was a whole different matter. If Chase was innocent, then was her faith in the team misplaced? Or was she wrong to believe the man now standing in front of her?

Neither option was a comforting one.

* * *

MILITARY K-9 UNIT:

These soldiers track down a serial killer with the help of their brave canine partners

Mission to Protect–Terri Reed, April 2018
Bound by Duty–Valerie Hansen, May 2018
Top Secret Target–Dana Mentink, June 2018
Standing Fast–Maggie K. Black, July 2018
Rescue Operation–Lenora Worth, August 2018
Explosive Force–Lynette Eason, September 2018
Battle Tested–Laura Scott, October 2018
Valiant Defender–Shirlee McCoy, November 2018
Military K-9 Unit Christmas–Valerie Hansen and Laura Scott, December 2018

Maggie K. Black is an award-winning journalist and romantic suspense author with an insatiable love of traveling the world. She has lived in the American South, Europe and the Middle East. She now makes her home in Canada with her history-teacher husband, their two beautiful girls and a small but mighty dog. Maggie enjoys connecting with her readers at maggiekblack.com.

Books by Maggie K. Black

Love Inspired Suspense

Military K-9 Unit

Standing Fast

True North Heroes

Undercover Holiday Fiancée
The Littlest Target

True North Bodyguards

Kidnapped at Christmas
Rescue at Cedar Lake
Protective Measures

Killer Assignment
Deadline
Silent Hunter
Headline: Murder
Christmas Blackout
Tactical Rescue

Visit the Author Profile page at Harlequin.com.

STANDING FAST

MAGGIE K. BLACK

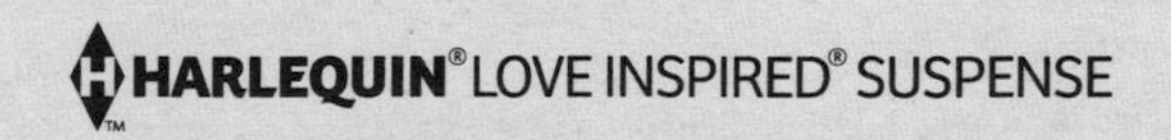

Special thanks and acknowledgment are given to Maggie K. Black for her contribution to the Military K-9 Unit miniseries.

Recycling programs for this product may not exist in your area.

LOVE INSPIRED BOOKS

ISBN-13: 978-1-335-54385-1

Standing Fast

This edition published by arrangement with Love Inspired Books.

www.Harlequin.com

Printed in U.S.A.

Wherefore take unto you the whole armor of God,
that ye may be able to withstand in the evil day,
and having done all, to stand.

—*Ephesians* 6:13

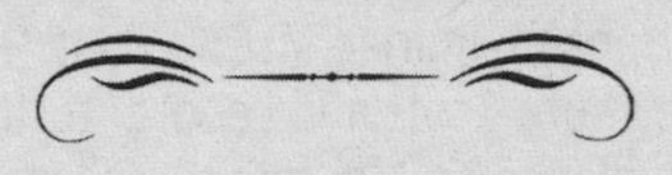

Thank you to my wonderful editor, Emily Rodmell, for including me in this, my first continuity series. Thanks as always to my agent, Melissa Jeglinski, who discussed series writing with me over chicken Parmesan.

Also, huge amounts of gratitude to Lynette Eason, Valerie Hansen, Shirlee McCoy, Dana Mentink, Terri Reed, Laura Scott and Lenora Worth for your support, guidance and friendship as I was crafting this book. I'm honored to write alongside you.

ONE

The scream was high-pitched and terrified, shattering the muggy darkness of predawn July and sending Senior Airman Chase McLear shooting straight out of bed like a bullet from a gun before he'd even fully woken up. Furious howls from his K-9 beagle, Queenie, sounded the alarm that danger was near. Chase's long legs propelled him across the floor, clad in gray track pant civvies. He felt the muscles in his arms tense for an unknown battle, as the faces of the brave men and women who'd been viciously killed by Boyd Sullivan, the notorious Red Rose Killer, flickered like a slideshow through his mind.

Help me catch him, Lord, and end the fear that's gripped the base!

Sudden pain shot through his sole as his bare foot landed hard on one of the wooden building blocks his daughter, Allie, had left scattered across the floor. He grabbed the door frame and blinked hard. His eyes struggled to focus on shapes in the darkness as his throbbing foot yanked him back to consciousness.

He was standing in the bedroom doorway of his modest Canyon Air Force Base bungalow. A humid breeze slipped in through the thick screen at the very bottom of his bedroom window where he'd left it ajar just a couple of inches to save using electricity on air-conditioning. The clock read twenty after five in the morning. His three-year-old daughter was crying out in her sleep from her bedroom down the hall.

Seemed they were both having nightmares tonight.

He started down the hall toward her, ignoring the stinging pain in his foot. The beagle's howls faded to a low warning growl, which he suspected meant in Queenie's mind the danger had passed. Had she just been howling because of Allie's cries?

"No!" His daughter's tiny panicked voice filled the darkened air. "Bad man! Hurt man! No!"

His brow creased. "Bad man" and "hurt man" were common themes in his daughter's nightmares these days. He wasn't sure why. Her preschool teacher, Maisy Lockwood, had assured him that many parents on base had told her their children had been having nightmares since Boyd had broken out of prison, killed several people and released hundreds of dogs from the K-9 kennels back in April.

But he'd done everything in his power to protect Allie from hearing anything about it—including the fact that because someone had apparently used his name when they visited Boyd before he escaped prison, Chase had been recently questioned as a suspect. It had been a little over three weeks since Air Force Investigations had first put him through the ringer, questioning his alibi for the night Boyd had broken onto the base. They seemed determined to pick a hole in Chase's story that he'd been on a video call with a buddy he'd worked with in Afghanistan at the time. Even he had to admit the fact that he couldn't provide the investigators with the video logs didn't exactly make him look innocent. But his laptop had been stolen from his truck early the next morning, along with his toolbox and gym bag. He just had to hope the investigators would corroborate his alibi soon and realize they'd targeted the wrong man. He'd been doing a whole lot of praying in the meantime.

"It's okay, Allie! Everything's going to

be okay. Daddy's coming!" He reached her room. There in the gentle glow of a night-light was his daughter's tiny form tossing and turning on top of her blankets. Her eyes were still scrunched tightly in sleep. His heart swelled with love for the little girl who'd brought such unexpected joy into his life. His voice dropped softly. "Hey, it's okay. Daddy's here. You're safe."

As he took a step toward her, his toes brushed something warm and soft in the darkness. A wet tongue licked his heel. He crouched down and felt Queenie's small furry head under his fingertips. It had been just a few months since he and the electronic-sniffing dog had started training together, and already Queenie had attached herself to him and Allie as if she'd always been a member of their small, fractured family.

"Good dog," he whispered, wondering how it would look to someone from the outside world to see a man who stood almost six foot four crouched down in a purple room with his arms spread between two such tiny beings, both of whom, in their own way, tugged on his heartstrings. Allie had been the one person who had given his life meaning and purpose after her mother, Liz, had shattered his heart, falling for another man and then filing for divorce while he was deployed in Afghanistan. And the small beagle at his feet represented the fresh start the K-9 unit would bring to his Security Forces career. He'd had enough of shipping off overseas to guard weapons transfers and depots in Afghanistan. It had been time to take on a different type of air force law enforcement work and become the kind of father his daughter needed him to be.

But now, it could all be snatched away. Someone who'd been accused of helping Boyd terrorize the K-9 unit, endanger the dogs and kill two trainers had no place in the kennels. So just three weeks before he and Queenie were due to graduate, their training had been put on hold while investigators decided whether to charge him or clear his name. He was just thankful Master Sergeant Caleb Streeter had allowed him to continue training with Queenie at home. The bond between trainer and dog was at a vital stage, and if they'd broken it now, Queenie might have had to have been retrained again from the start. Maybe she'd have even been reassigned to a different partner.

A loud crack outside yanked his attention to the window at his right. He leaped to his feet and started for the glass just in time to see the blur of a figure rush away through the bushes. His heart pounded like a war drum in his rib cage as he threw open the window. The screen had been slit with what looked like a knife and peeled back, as if someone had tried to get inside. He mentally kicked himself for assuming Queenie had been howling about Allie's nightmares and for not doing a sweep of the room when he ran in earlier. But his focus had been on one thing—his little girl.

Lord, please help me be the man she needs to protect her!

He closed the window firmly, locking it in place, and cast another glance at where his daughter lay sleeping peacefully. Then he looked down at Queenie. "Stay here. Protect Allie."

He left the dog curled up beside his daughter, ran back down the hall to his bedroom, pulled his Beretta M9 pistol from his bedside safe and slid a pair of running shoes on over his bare feet. Then he stepped out the back door, locking it behind him. The sky was dark, with only a sliver of pink brushing the horizon. He moved slowly and carefully around the side of the house toward his daughter's window. There was no one there. But the footprints that scuffed the ground made it clear that somebody had been. Jagged edges of the screen ran from one side of Allie's window to the other, like an ugly wound. Presumably, the dog's howls had scared the prowler away. A prayer of thanksgiving for the small dog filled his heart.

As he moved away, something crunched under his feet. He bent down.

Half of the cherished macaroni-and-cardboard framed picture of Allie with her teacher, Maisy, was lying in the dirt. The picture that had been on his daughter's dresser just hours ago. Whoever had slit the screen had reached in, grabbed the picture and torn it in half, ripping off the part of the photo with Allie on it and leaving just the preschool teacher's image behind. Horror poured down his spine like ice. Someone had grabbed a picture of his daughter. But why? Who would possibly target his little girl? Boyd Sullivan, the Red Rose Killer, killed only those who he'd felt had wronged him in some way. Chase's precious daughter was an innocent.

He held the damaged picture up to the glow of his back porch light. Maisy's blue eyes sparkled up at him, filled with a happiness and energy that had only been matched by that of the little girl whom she'd held tightly in her arms. Petite and bubbly, with a spunky blond pixie haircut, Maisy had first caught his eye several years before he'd met Liz, when he'd been suffering through basic training under her notoriously tough father, who had been head of basic military training. At the time, so much as saying a quick "Howdy" to Chief Master Sergeant Clint Lockwood's daughter would've gotten him more laps around the track than he'd been willing to risk. He thought he'd gotten over his foolish attraction to Maisy when he'd been deployed overseas, met Liz and settled into the rut of their unhappy marriage. Still, he couldn't deny the fact that ever since coming back to Texas, the sight of Maisy's smile still made those tattered corners of his good-for-nothing heart flutter something fierce.

The fact that his motherless little girl clearly adored her made that all the stronger.

He recalled the panicked news that had filtered through the base the morning of April 1, when Boyd had broken out of jail and continued his terrifying crusade against those he felt had wronged him. In addition to taking the lives of two trainers, he'd murdered Maisy's father in apparent revenge for having once washed him out of basic training. That night, something had unexpectedly pounded so hard in Chase's chest that he'd wanted to run through the base to find Maisy, scoop her up into his arms and promise he'd do anything in his power to avenge her father's death. Instead, a nod and an "I'm sorry for your loss" at the Sunny Seeds Preschool gate had had to do.

Sudden footsteps sounded in the darkness. Bright light shone in his eyes. Voices shouted so loudly they seemed to be coming from all directions at once. "Hands up! Hands up! Get down! Down on the ground!"

Six members of the Air Force Emergency Services team swarmed his yard in full flak gear. Someone must have seen either him or the prowler in the bushes and called the police. Instinctively, he dropped to his knees and put his hands up as instructed, with his gun in one hand and the picture in the other.

"Hey, guys! It's okay! This is my house. There was a prowler, but they're gone!"

"Hands where we can see them, Airman!" The voice was brusque and male.

Chase complied. What was going on? True, he'd only been stationed back at the base for a little over a year, and before starting K-9 training, most of his Security Forces work had involved things like guarding gates and patrolling secure facilities. But that didn't change the fact that these men and women in uniform were still his colleagues. He searched past the barrels of M4 carbine rifles and Berretta M9 pistols for a familiar face. From inside the house, he could hear Queenie barking. Allie's wails rose. Cops rushed past him, kicking down his front door to get inside and fanning out around his small home.

"Clear!" voices echoed from inside his home.

"Clear!" came another.

What was this? What were they searching for?

"Let me explain," he said, in the calmest voice he could muster. "There was a prowler. But they're gone."

No response. His teeth clenched. His heartbeat roared. Enough was enough! They were terrifying Allie, and for what? "Please! Let me go get my daughter!"

A sigh of relief filled Chase's lungs as the tall form of Captain Justin Blackwood, head of the Boyd Sullivan investigation, stepped around the corner. Blackwood's reputation as a stellar cop was beyond reproach.

"Sir!" Chase said, instinctively feeling his shoulders straighten and his fingers flinch, wanting to salute. "What's going on?"

But any relief he'd felt melted away as he saw the grim frown on the captain's face.

"Airman Chase McLear. We have a warrant to search your premises. We have reason to believe you're harboring Boyd Sullivan."

Faint hues of crimson and burnt orange sky brushed along the edges of the horizon as Maisy Lockwood jogged down the sidewalk and through the residential neighborhoods of Canyon Air Force Base. Water sloshed back and forth in her metal water bottle as it knocked around inside the backpack that sat heavy on her slender shoulders. The sun had just started its climb into the morning sky, but already she could smell the humidity in the air. Today was going to be another scorcher.

The whole base is on high alert and you're out jogging alone? The voice of her close friend and newlywed Staff Sergeant Felicity James filled her mind.

At least I'm not wearing headphones, she mentally argued back. As much as she missed pounding her sneakers down the pavement in time to the music, running without it was one of the many changes she'd made since Boyd Sullivan had escaped prison and broken onto the base to kill those his twisted mind thought had somehow wronged him. But giving up jogging around the base before heading into work at Sunny Seeds Preschool each morning, just like she had with her father every day for years before he was murdered, had been one thing she'd refused to let that demented killer take from her.

Something inside her needed that time to pray, and sometimes even cry, before opening the classroom doors each morning and welcoming the shining, hopeful little faces who counted on her to be the caring one who doled out hugs, wiped away tears and blew air kisses over bumped foreheads and scraped knees. They needed her to be at her best. So she mourned for the father whose approval she'd never quite managed to earn, knowing with each step that maybe if she'd gotten there just a few minutes earlier on the morning he was murdered by Boyd, he'd still be alive.

She blinked back a tear and tightened the pink bandanna that held back her hair. Her father's basic training officer voice thundered through her ears. *I'm not here to baby anybody's feelings or hold anybody's hand. There are two types of people in the world, the weak and the strong. Which one are you?*

Weak. That was his implication. Just like her beautiful and delicate mother who'd died from a drug overdose when Maisy was thirteen, leaving her in the care of a man who didn't do hugs and definitely wasn't about to blow an air kiss over any of life's wounds. At barely five feet tall, with two left feet, Clint Lockwood's only child hadn't even tried to take the air force's physical test, much to his disappointment. A sudden lump formed in her throat. Their relationship hadn't been perfect, true, but when Boyd had murdered him, he'd taken not only his life but Maisy's hope that their relationship could ever be better. She swallowed hard. Her father had considered Boyd weak too. And the angry and disturbed young man had returned the day he'd escaped prison to get his revenge.

Red-and-blue lights flashed ahead. The sound of sirens mingled with the fierce sound of fearless K-9 dogs barking. Security Forces cops in combat gear swarmed a small bungalow. Her breath caught. Had police finally caught Boyd or the accomplice who'd been sneaking him on and off the base?

Please, Lord, may the nightmare finally be over. Help them catch Boyd before anybody else gets hurt!

As she approached the police operation, her footsteps faltered. There was someone ahead of her, crouched low in the bushes, watching the police operation.

They had their back to her and their features were obscured by an oversize hoodie and a black baseball cap. The figure seemed too slender to be Boyd. Could it be Boyd's accomplice? Was it the anonymous blogger who'd been making people's lives miserable with a steady stream of salacious gossip? Or even some paranoid Canyon resident who thought they needed to skulk in the shadows and disguise themselves to avoid the Red Rose Killer?

Maisy's pulse quickened. She reached into her pocket, feeling for her cell phone.

The figure turned. A bandanna covered the lower half of their face. A knife flashed in their gloved hand.

Save me, Lord!

Instantly, she whipped her backpack off her shoulders and spun it around in front of her like a defensive shield. A heavy metal water bottle wasn't much against a knife, but one way or another she'd go down fighting. Her eyes searched in vain for a glimpse of the figure's eyes or anything solid to identify who they were.

"Stop right there!" she yelled, wincing at the way her own voice quaked. "Drop the knife! Right now! I mean it!"

The figure hesitated. Maisy's limbs shook.

Help me, Lord! What do I do?

She wasn't authorized to carry a weapon on base and the backpack wouldn't do much. But there were large rocks encircling a nearby garden and she had a whistle on her key chain. Whatever it took, no daughter of Clint Lockwood was going down without a fight. The barking of Canyon's K-9 dogs seemed to be growing louder, followed by the sound of even more sirens.

The figure lurched forward a step. Hot tears rushed to Maisy's eyes as she steadied herself to fight. Then the figure turned and sprinted away through the base.

Relief washed over Maisy's body and tension fled her limbs so suddenly she felt her knees go weak, nearly pitching her to the ground. Who was that? Had that knife been for protection or violence? She propelled her wobbly legs toward the cops, as her heart beat so hard in her slender frame. In the three and a half months since the Red Rose Killer had broken out of prison, it was like a deep fog of uncertainty and fear had descended over the base. Neighbors suspected neighbors. Colleagues viewed each other with suspicion. Stamping out gossip among her students was a daily task, and when parents arrived at the school, they hugged their children closer and were slower to let them go. Two of her friends, Felicity and Zoe, had quickly married the men of their dreams, rather than waiting a moment longer to start their happily-ever-afters. It was like everyone was a little more aware of how precious life could be.

Something crunched under her feet. She bent down. Her fingers reached for the glittering shapes, cupping them into her palms. They were seashells. No. Wait. They were dried pasta. Bright pink with gold paint splotches and coated in purple glitter, they were the same kind of pasta she used for craft time at Sunny Seeds, and unless she was very wrong, she'd helped one of her own students paint these very shells herself before painstakingly placing them on a cardboard picture frame—*Allie McLear.*

What would remnants of little Allie's treasured frame be doing out here on the ground? Confusion gripped her heart again as the bright-eyed toddler's face swam unbidden into her mind, along with that of her handsome, broad-shouldered father, Chase McLear. The students had made the frames and taken them home as a Valentine's Day present for their parents and caregivers. She could still remember the sweet and chagrined look on Chase's face the next day as he'd stood with his lanky form half leaning against the door frame to the entrance of Sunny Seeds and explained that Allie would like a picture of herself and Maisy to put in it, if she'd be okay with him taking one. She hadn't been about to say no.

She'd always tried her best not to have favorites, but she had to admit that Allie had burrowed a meaningful place in Maisy's heart. There was something special about the tiny blonde, motherless bundle of sunshine with vulnerable eyes and an eager smile. And if she was honest, she suspected Allie's father was something special too.

While he'd told her that he was one of thousands of airmen who'd been trained by her father, she hadn't actually met Chase before he'd been deployed to Afghanistan many years ago or spoken to him until he moved back to Texas and enrolled his daughter in Sunny Seeds. She'd vowed long ago that she'd never fall for a man in uniform. It was a promise she'd stuck to for all twenty-five years of her life. But she couldn't deny that over the past few months she'd developed a bit of a crush on Allie's father. Probably ever since the day the single father had first dropped Allie off in her care.

Her steps quickened as she recognized the house number and street from the Sunny

Seeds's attendance records. Police encircled Chase and Allie's house. Were they in some kind of trouble? Had they been targeted by the Red Rose Killer? *Please, no!*

She started running toward the house. A small crowd of people had formed on the sidewalk. She pushed past them, her heart stuttering a beat as she caught sight of the tall and strong form of her friend Captain Justin Blackwood standing among the cops. What was the head of the Red Rose Killer investigation doing at Allie and Chase's house? She ran for him. She had to tell him about the knife-wielding figure.

A hand in the crowd caught her arm. She turned back. It was the tall, blonde form of Yvette Crenville, the base nutritionist and someone else who she knew had been targeted and threatened by Boyd Sullivan thanks to a failed past romance.

"We've got to stay back," Yvette said. She let go of Maisy's arm. "They're making an arrest. It might be Boyd's accomplice."

"Thanks for the warning," Maisy said. She prayed Chase and Allie were all right. "I just saw a prowler in the bushes. I have to report it while there might still be a chance to catch them."

"Could it be Boyd?" Yvette's beautiful eyes

went wide. "Someone reported that he was seen going in and out of that house."

Chase and Allie's house? "No, that's not possible. One of my students lives there. Her father seems like a really great guy. There's no way..."

Her voice trailed off, unable to find the words to finish the sentence. After all, Yvette had never expected that the man she'd once loved would turn out to be a serial killer. She ran toward Justin, even as she felt her gaze pull toward the house. Two cops flanked a tall and broad-shouldered man in soft gray track pants and a simple white T-shirt who knelt by the back door of the bungalow. His head was bowed and his hands were linked on top of his head.

Chase looked up, and his eyes widened as his gaze met hers through the chaos, and the previous stutter she'd felt in her chest turned into a jolt so painful it seemed to shock her heart's ability to even beat.

No, no it couldn't be. Her secret crush, and the single father of her favorite student, was being arrested for harboring her father's killer.

TWO

Maisy watched, her head swimming in confusion and disbelief, as Chase stayed kneeling between the uniformed cops. Prayer filled her aching chest.

Lord, what's happening? Did Chase really have something to do with Dad's murder?

"Justin!"

The tall cop turned toward her, his lips set in a grim line. "Morning, Maisy. I've got to ask you to step back."

Justin Blackwood was a tough and reliable captain, but even then, she'd never seen his face so serious.

"I just saw a prowler in the bushes with a knife!" she said, forcing herself to leave the question of Chase's arrest for now. If there was even a possibility it was Boyd Sullivan, that was all that mattered for now. She pointed. "Over there. I couldn't tell if it was a man or a woman. But they were thin. I don't think it was Boyd Sullivan, but he's been living in the woods for months, so who knows how much weight he's lost. They had a hoodie and a bandanna over their face. They pulled a knife, but when I yelled they ran away. I think they had part of a picture frame Allie and I made."

She held out her hand to show him the pieces she'd picked up. Justin's face paled. In an instant he'd summoned two K-9 officers to his side and quickly took a detailed description of the suspect's appearance from Maisy and the direction he'd gone. The cops and their canine partners took off after the suspect. Justin turned to Maisy.

"Are you okay?" Concern reverberated through his voice.

She nodded as something about the sincerity of her friend's caring question made her voice catch. The single father of a teenaged girl, Justin had been someone Maisy had considered a friend for years. If she was honest, she suspected her father had been disappointed that no romantic spark had ever bloomed between her and the military police captain. She'd definitely noticed how the cut of Justin's jaw and the intensity of his gaze had a certain attractiveness, which had turned more than one female head on base. But the fact that his obvious good looks had never had any impact on her personally had been one of the reasons she figured she was immune to the charms of any man in uniform—a thought that had promptly evaporated the moment Chase McLear had brought little Allie into Sunny Seeds and sent a thousand butterfly wings flapping in Maisy's chest.

"I'm okay," she said. "They didn't threaten me or come anywhere near touching me. They just pulled a knife and then ran. Whoever they were, I wasn't their target."

Justin nodded slowly. She had a pretty good guess what he was thinking. In the several sightings of the Red Rose Killer since he'd escaped prison, one constant that remained was that he only killed people he thought deserved it—*like her father*—or that he needed something from to achieve that aim.

"What's going on?" she demanded. "Why are you arresting Chase McLear? Yvette said Boyd had been seen going in and out of his house. That can't be true."

He paused and his eyes rose to the sky as if he was trying to decide what to tell her.

"I know that different members of the investigative team have been chasing down a lot of different leads," she added quickly. "I don't expect to be kept in the loop about all of them and I know there's a lot you can't tell me. But Chase is the father of one of my students."

Justin's brows furrowed and for a moment, it looked like he was weighing his words before deciding what to say. "I can confirm that the investigative team received an anonymous tip that Chase McLear was harboring the Red Rose Killer—"

"But that's impossible!" Maisy felt her hand rise to her lips. "Chase… I mean, Senior Airman McLear is a good man and a devoted father."

A single eyebrow rose. "I assume this is your subjective personal opinion of the man from your interactions with him and not based on any specific evidence as to his relationship with Boyd Sullivan?"

Heat rose to her face. If she was honest, she wasn't even sure why she was defending Chase so quickly and eagerly. There was just something about him that got to her. She'd always believed in Jesus's teaching from "The Sermon on the Mount" that the true character of a person's heart was known by the things he did. Despite his reserved exterior, she was convinced Chase truly loved his daughter. It was obvious every time she'd watched Allie barrel into his waiting arms at the end of the day. And sometimes when he met her gaze over his daughter's blond curls, it was almost like she caught a glimpse of something lost and broken behind his deep green eyes.

"Senior Airman McLear says it was all a misunderstanding and that there was a prowler on his property—"

"And I saw a prowler with a knife," Maisy interjected again. The slight narrowing of her friend's eyes suddenly reminded her that as a friend and civilian she was being treated with far more latitude than anyone serving under the strict captain would have ever received for such an outburst. "I'm sorry. That was rude. I'm just really shaken by this."

"I understand," he said, but the firm timber of his voice let her know just how little impact her passionate defense of Chase would have on his investigation. "Senior Airman McLear has maintained his innocence. We will of course be taking his claims of a prowler seriously and hopefully my officers will be able to track down and catch the person you saw. I'm trusting you to respect the fact that there is additional information about this investigation that I'm not at liberty to tell you. But I do feel a responsibility to let you know this is not the first time this suspect has come to our attention. Now, I have to ask you, do you know if he had any kind of relationship or interaction with your father?"

"No." She shook her head, feeling her sweat-soaked hair dance and fly around her head. "My dad was his basic training officer, but that was years ago."

"Do you know if your father was particularly hard on him?" the captain pressed.

"My father was hard on a lot of people." Especially her. Again, her eyes flicked to where Chase was kneeling, flanked by officers. Anger burned in his eyes, mixed with a quiet desperation bordering on panic, like a wounded animal desperately scanning the snare that had just trapped him. "Look, Chase can't be working with Boyd Sullivan. I'm almost certain of it."

The lines of Justin's brow furrowed deeper. "Again, do you have any evidence to back that up?"

"No." Her chest fell. She had a hunch and nothing more.

Was her blind faith of Chase's true nature any different than Yvette's had been about Boyd?

A frightened and furious wail seemed to break through the early morning air and rise above the chaos. A cop in flak gear was carrying a squirming and pajama-clad Allie out of the house. She recognized him. Lieutenant Preston Flannigan was the slightly pushy single father of one of the boys in her preschool.

"No!" Allie squirmed, fighting against the firm arms holding her. "Stop! No! I want Daddy!"

Sudden tears rushed to Maisy's eyes. "What's going to happen to Allie?"

"That's up to Chase. We'll be taking him in for questioning. Hopefully, he has someone who can take her. If not, we'll arrange for a base social worker."

A stranger? She knew the social workers on base were wonderful people who did a difficult job, but still, she couldn't imagine how hard it would be on little Allie to understand where she was going and what was happening to her. She glanced at Chase. His face had paled with an agony that seemed to rip her own heart in half. No, she couldn't just stand there and watch this happen. She took a step toward the little girl. "Allie, it's going to be okay."

Allie's tearstained face turned toward her. "Maisy! I want Miss Maisy!"

Her little arms shot out, and Maisy felt her arms instinctively wrap around the child.

"Justin, I'll take her to the preschool with me, if Chase is okay with that. She's one of my students and watching her the extra hour before school starts is no trouble at all. I know her and she knows me."

Concern rumbled in the captain's voice. "Are you sure?"

Maisy's eyes glanced from father to daughter. "Absolutely."

"All right." He led her through the crowd until they reached Chase. "Maisy has offered to take care of your daughter while you come in for questioning. Is that acceptable to you?"

Chase turned toward them and gratitude filled his gaze. "Yes, thank you. Please, don't let her out of your sight. There was a prowler outside of my home this morning. They cut the screen on her bedroom window."

Was that the same person she'd seen skulking in the bushes? She wanted to ask him more and tell him what she'd seen, but with Security Forces all around and little frightened Allie in her arms it would have to wait. "I'll keep her safe, Chase. I promise."

"Thanks," he said again. "She'll need to get dressed and changed. Plus, I haven't fed her breakfast yet. She's recently been refusing to eat cereal if milk touches it, but she's okay with fruit..." His voice trailed off, as if his mind was struggling to figure out what else he should tell her.

"Don't worry," she said quickly. "I've got a change of clothes for her in her cubby at the preschool. I bought some fresh fruit yesterday and I have frozen waffles and yogurt on hand for breakfast."

The number of students who'd been having problems both eating and sleeping had increased since the Red Rose Killer had broken onto the base. She heard Allie's babbling voice at her ear, and the toddler took Maisy's face in both of her hands, turning the preschool teacher's gaze away from Chase. Allie looked at her seriously. "Police broke my house, Maisy."

"The police are just searching your house to make sure that you and your daddy are okay," Maisy said, softly. "Like Queenie searches your house for things. Now, your daddy is going to help the police and you are going to come to school with me. We'll have special strawberries and waffles for breakfast. Would you like that?"

Allie stuck her lip out. "Queenie comes too?"

Maisy looked down. A young beagle sat by her ankle. It looked up protectively at Allie in a way that told her that she wouldn't be able to shake the dog, even if she wanted to. "Yes, of course. Queenie can come too."

"Queenie likes waffles." Allie tucked her head against Maisy's chest and she felt the young girl shudder in the safety of her arms.

Chase met her eyes over Allie's head again. "Thank you."

"No problem. We'll see you later."

The pink-and-orange glow of a Texas dawn had deepened over the horizon. The first parents would be at the preschool ready to drop their kids off in a little over an hour. She started to turn away when she heard Justin calling her name. She looked back. The captain was striding toward them. Something glittered in his gloved hand. It was a sturdy gold cross, dangling on the end of a chain.

He stretched the pendant toward her. "Before you go, one of our officers just found this buried under the floorboards in Chase's house. I was wondering if you could identify it?"

Her blood ran cold as suddenly as if she'd just plunged into ice. She nodded. Her mouth opened, but for a moment, no words came out. Justin Blackwood turned the cross over and the early morning light fell on the engraved words she'd so carefully chosen as a teenager years ago. *I love you, Dad—Maisy.*

Her heart sank to a place that was worse than disappointment or even sadness. "Yes, that's the cross I gave my father for Christmas when I was thirteen, a few months after my mother died. Despite our differences, he wore it under his uniform and never took it off. When the Red Rose Killer murdered him, somebody stole it from his body."

She could almost feel Chase's gaze on her face, but she forced herself to turn away without meeting his eye. She didn't even begin to know what to think. But the fact that it had now shown up in Chase McLear's home made it a lot harder to hold on to the faint hope that the father of the little girl she now held in her arms wasn't somehow linked to his murder.

"Stephen Butler, commissary cook!" Preston slapped the glossy photo of the corpse of one of the Red Rose Killer's most recent victims down on the interrogation table in front of Chase. "Found dead behind a restaurant off base. Boyd Sullivan used his uniform and ID to sneak onto base after escaping prison. Did you lure him to the woods for Boyd? Are you responsible for this man's murder?"

"No, sir." Chase's jaw ached and his lower back twinged with the reminder that he hadn't stood or stretched in hours. But he wasn't about to let his bearing relax. They'd brought him in for questioning in the same track pants and T-shirt he'd been wearing when they'd arrested him. Being challenged by uniformed men while in his civvies made the humiliation he felt even worse. But he wasn't about to give in to the temptation to slouch.

An airman was an airman, even out of uniform.

His eyes roamed over the glossy picture of the dead young man. The Red Rose Killer's first set of victims before his arrest had been linked by a common thread—they were all people who'd treated him worse than he felt he'd deserved. A homecoming queen who'd broken his heart, a high school bully and a gas station attendant who'd fired him had been the first three people he had killed. A woman he'd once dated and her new boyfriend rounded out the five murders that he'd gone to prison for. But since breaking out of prison, his targets had been more mixed. Some seemed to be revenge killings, complete with a red rose and a note left on the body. Others, like poor Stephen Butler, seemed to have been killed for practical reasons, like gaining access to the base or the kennels. Preston had already covered the first set of victims and had now moved onto crimes committed since Boyd had broken out of prison.

Captain Justin Blackwood stood stone-faced and impassive by the door, apparently content to watch as Preston conducted the questioning with the volume and aggression of an angry terrier that had cornered a rat. Chase wasn't sure what that meant. Was the captain not as convinced of his guilt as the lieutenant was? He could only hope that the forensic team was taking the cut in Allie's window screen, the torn picture and the footsteps in the dirt as seriously as Security Forces were taking their investigation into him.

When Lieutenant Ethan Webb had met him in a coffee shop three and a half weeks ago and told him his name had shown up on Boyd Sullivan's prison visitor list, Chase had been both shocked and indignant; his frustration at just how ludicrous the whole situation was had shown in both his tone of voice and his body language. He still kicked himself for that. Growing up, his grandfather, Senior Master Sergeant Donald McLear, had drilled into him that a man and a hero always kept his chin high and his emotions in check. But the idea that he'd do anything to help Boyd Sullivan had been both insulting and laughable. How could anyone think he'd want to spend one minute in the presence of that monster? He'd expected his name would be cleared immediately and that whoever had used his name to cover their tracks had picked him at random. Even the fact that his laptop had been stolen from his truck, along with his gym bag and toolbox, had seemed like a cruel coincidence.

But any hope that he wasn't being personally targeted, which had remained flickering in his heart, was completely snuffed out the second Captain Blackwood had held the late Chief Master Sergeant Clint Lockwood's gold cross in Maisy's startled face. The thought that it had been found under his living room floorboards chilled him to the bone. He'd been set up, no doubt about it, by someone who'd both been inside his home and had eyes on his truck. He didn't know who and he didn't know why. But one thing was certain—for the sake of his little girl, he had to clear his name.

"Landon Martelli and Tamara Peterson," Preston barked, as he slammed the pictures of two more of Sullivan's victims down on the table. "Both were K-9 trainers and murdered by someone who opened the kennel doors, letting about two hundred dogs go free. You don't have an alibi for the morning this happened, do you?"

Chase fought the urge to cross his arms. "As I've stated before, I was on a video chat with a military contractor named Ajay Joseph, who I used to work with in Afghanistan, from four fifteen in the morning until my cell phone rang shortly after oh five hundred with an alert that Boyd Sullivan had escaped prison and let dogs loose on base. I paused the video call and went into the bedroom to answer my cell phone and spoke to Master Sergeant Westley James. When I returned to the living room, approximately eight minutes later, my daughter, Allie, was up and playing with Queenie and the video call had ended."

"But you have no way to corroborate that story," Preston interjected.

"That I was at home and on a video call when Sullivan broke onto base? No, I don't. Because my laptop was stolen, along with my gym bag and toolbox, from my truck when I was off base and I haven't been able to reach my contact."

Preston smirked. Yeah, Chase knew how weak his alibi sounded. It didn't help that he hadn't been able to reach Ajay since then. But he was an Afghan, an independent contractor and a coordinator between locals and the United States Air Force. Ajay wasn't stationed on base, and off-base communication in his part of Afghanistan had been unstable.

"Two dozen of the dogs Boyd let out of the kennels still haven't been found, Airman," Preston said. "Many of them had PTSD from serving their country and saving the lives of service members overseas. You recently transferred to the K-9 unit, didn't you?"

Was it his imagination or did Chase pick up a hint of resentment in the lieutenant's voice. It was no secret that Preston had done basic K-9 training as well but had yet to be paired with a canine partner. Did he resent that Chase had been partnered first? He hadn't thought so. He'd have expected a man like Preston to be focused on getting a fierce and dangerous animal, who specialized in something like suspect apprehension, rather than a sweet little search dog like Queenie.

"Yes, sir, I did request a transfer to the K-9 unit," Chase said. "Though, as I'm sure you know, completion of my training with the team is currently on hold until this mix-up can be resolved. I have the utmost respect for what the dogs in the unit and their trainers do to serve our great country. I hope the missing dogs are found soon."

"I spoke to your old boss, Captain Reardon," Preston said, "and she described you as a quiet man who kept to himself."

Chase didn't answer. He hadn't been asked a question and didn't like Preston's insinuation that being private and quiet was somehow a crime.

"Why did you request a transfer?" Justin's voice snapped his attention to the doorway. Chase blinked. He couldn't remember the lead investigator asking any other questions since the interrogation had started. "Your previous career was security, correct? You guarded missiles, weapons transfers and installations in Afghanistan?"

"And personnel, yes, sir," Chase said. "I requested a transfer because as fulfilling as it was to be overseas, serving my country on the front line, I couldn't neglect my duty to my own daughter. Seeing the difference we were making in the lives of Afghan children made me miss my own. I figured my daughter deserved better in life than a daddy who she knew only through a video-chat screen, sir."

Justin's eyebrows rose. His mouth opened, like he was about to ask a follow-up question, and Chase suddenly remembered that Justin himself was the single father of a teenaged daughter.

The sound of another picture smacking the table yanked Chase's attention back to Preston. He looked down and his heart ached. It was Maisy's father, Chief Master Sergeant Clint Lockwood, lying on the floor in a navy blue PT uniform. A red rose was tucked under his arm. A dark pool of blood stained his crisp white shirt.

Maisy thinks I had something to do with this? Anger and sadness crashed over Chase like competing waves battling on the shore. The look of disbelief and doubt in her eyes when she'd looked at the gold cross was seared in his mind. It reminded him all too much of the look of defeat that had greeted him when he'd answered the overseas video call from his then pregnant wife, telling him that she'd given up on their marriage and fallen in love with another man who was "emotionally available" for her in a way Chase could never be. Liz had filed for divorce almost immediately. Thankfully a DNA test after Allie was born had proven she was Chase's little girl. Even before Allie was born, Liz had decided to restart her life without them.

"Chief Master Sergeant Lockwood was my basic training officer," Chase said, quickly, snapping his errant mind back to attention and filling in the information before Preston could try to hit him with another question. “It’s well-known by everyone who trained under him how tough he could be. He didn’t give me a rougher time than anybody else, and I certainly didn’t hold a grudge.”

Before Preston could speak, Justin asked another question. “What’s your relationship like with his daughter, Maisy Lockwood?”

“Much the same as I imagine Lieutenant Flannigan’s is, sir,” Chase said. “Polite and courteous, but not personal. My daughter is in her preschool, as his son is.”

Was it Chase’s imagination or did irritation flicker in Preston’s eyes?

“Then why were you holding a picture of her when you were arrested?” Preston snapped.

“I’ve already answered that question. There was a prowler outside my daughter’s window. I went outside to investigate and found the picture in the dirt. They cut the screen on Allie’s bedroom window, pulled the picture from her dresser and ripped my daughter’s face from the frame. My baby daughter’s picture is now in this person’s hands.”

He fought the urge to drop his head into his hands. Instead, his eyes rose to the ceiling as he prayed. Did they believe he’d cut the screen and scuffed the ground himself to cover his tracks in case someone saw Boyd near his home and called the police? Didn't they get how ridiculous that would be?

"My name was used by someone visiting the Red Rose Killer in prison," he added. "My truck was broken into. I was robbed. My home was invaded by someone who planted evidence under my floorboards. My daughter is in danger. I need to protect her. What you should be investigating is who is so intent on framing me."

A quick, curt knock sounded on the door, interrupting wherever Justin was going with his next question. Justin excused himself and slipped out into the hallway.

"I don't care what sack of lies you try to sell, I know you're helping Boyd Sullivan," Preston said. His lip curled. "A few scuffed footprints in the dirt and a hole in a window screen doesn't prove anything. You've been sneaking him on and off base. You helped him kill these people and I will prove it."

Chase felt his jaw clench. How could anyone possibly think he'd allow a man like Boyd in his home or near his daughter? He held his tongue and stared straight ahead as if Preston was nothing but a window and he was looking through him. Still, he couldn't miss the dangerous glint in the lieutenant's eyes.

A lifetime in the Security Forces had taught him to spot a hostile element.

The door handle began to turn and Preston leaned forward so suddenly the table lurched.

"You better stay far away from Maisy Lockwood," he hissed. "Take your little brat out of her school and never bother her again. Or I will make sure you pay."

THREE

The lead investigator walked back into the room, giving Chase barely a moment to process Preston's words before rising to his feet and saluting. Preston rose as well.

Justin's eyes scanned their faces. "Everything all right, men?"

"Yes, sir," Preston said.

Chase did his best to keep his face impassive. Preston's determination to nail him was immaterial. Chase knew he was innocent.

As if he read Chase's thoughts, Justin turned to him. "You're free to go."

So he wasn't being charged? Did that mean they didn't have enough evidence? Or did they think that if they let him go and trailed him, he'd eventually lead them to the Red Rose Killer?

"You are not being charged with any crime at the moment," Justin went on, his face so steady he might as well have been carved out of marble. "We may wish you to come in for future questioning and appreciate your continued voluntary cooperation with our investigation. JAG can inform you of your legal rights going forward, including your right to cease cooperation and retain legal counsel. Don't leave base without letting my office know. I believe the team has finished processing your home as well. You can collect your cell phone later this afternoon."

"Thank you, sir." Chase saluted sharply.

The other man returned the salute, and Chase was escorted from the building. But it wasn't until he stepped inside the front door of his own Canyon bungalow that he let his shoulders slump and his bearing relax. Twenty minutes later he was showered, shaved and dressed in his crisp dark blue uniform, with its pale blue shirt, navy tie and laces tight on the leather shoes that were so well shined he could almost see the mess of the house that surrounded him reflected in them. He'd need to have the front door replaced before Allie came home. It still opened and closed all right, but the visible dent and damaged hinges would upset her. His bedroom and the living room had both been tossed, but nothing seemed broken—he was thankful for that—and his daughter's room would only take a minute to set back to rights. Even the window screen would be easy enough to replace. He'd change the locks on the doors as well. A bigger problem would be repairing the baseboards and floor tiles. He'd carefully peeled back half a dozen of each to create little hiding places for electronic SD cards and thumb drives, as part of Queenie's training, and this had no doubt seemed suspicious enough for deeper investigation. Now, patches of his floor looked like a sloppy and haphazard contractor had quit partway through the job. He took another deep breath, let it out slowly and reminded himself that the investigators had only been doing their job. They'd done it with the utmost of respect and professionalism too—for the most part. He ran his hand over the back of his neck.

God, what do I do? Who's out to get me? How do I find them?

The red light on his answering machine was blinking. He pressed the button. The light and airy sound of Maisy's voice filled his wrecked and damaged living room, as sweet and as comforting as a chilled glass of sweet iced tea.

"Hey, Chase? It's Maisy. Not sure when you'll get this message, but Justin…uh, Captain Blackwood said you wouldn't have your cell phone. Allie wanted to give you a call to let you know we were having a good morning…" There was the sound of whispering and the scuffle of the phone changing hands.

Then he heard the voice of his daughter, Allie, sounding so tiny and little, and a sudden lump formed in his throat. "Hi, Daddy! Maisy let me have a special pink hair bow! And I had berries. And waffles. Queenie is here too. Say woof, Queenie! Queenie! Say woof, woof! Queenie doesn't want to say hi. Bye!"

There was the thump of the phone falling, another scuffling sound and a pause that lasted so long he wondered if they'd forgotten to hang up. Then he heard Maisy's voice again. There was an unmistakable strain of worry pressing through her light and cheerful tone. "Allie ate a lot of breakfast. She's good. Felicity gave me a scoop of dog food for Queenie. We're just going to hang out here and have a fun day. Give me a shout when you—"

The phone message cut off in a long beep. He sat down on the couch, feeling his heart beat hard against his rib cage. Then he played the message again, finding comfort in the sound of his daughter's voice and Maisy's reassurance. Did Maisy have any idea how much her act of kindness meant to him? His daughter had been screaming, his world had been falling apart and she'd been there for him, stepping into the chaos, reaching out her hands to his little girl, like a heroine plucking his daughter out of the rubble and into safety.

He'd never met a more beautiful, kind and generous woman.

Real men don't whimper and they don't complain. Nobody ever solved a problem by sitting around feeling sorry for themselves. Unexpectedly, his grandfather's voice echoed through the back of his mind. The Senior Master Sergeant had been in military intelligence long before Chase had been born and was proud of having gone to his grave never breathing a word of what his work had entailed. He'd been widowed when Chase was a baby, moved in with Chase and his parents and stepped into the role as head of the household, filling the void that was left behind by the hectic nature of his mother's long and exhausting overnight shifts as an ER nurse and his father's lengthy deployments overseas. He'd instilled in Chase at a young age that real men didn't lose control of their emotions, ever, even if they were four years old and had broken their leg jumping off the garage roof.

Chase gritted his teeth and stood up. This was no time for self-pity. Someone was out to get him, and he had to find out who. That was never going to happen while he was sitting around thinking about some pretty preschool teacher.

If Security Forces wasn't going to track down his alibi for the morning of the Red Rose Killer's murders, he was going to have to do it himself. The fact that Preston had brought up his former boss, Captain Jennifer Reardon, in the interrogation had reminded him that there might be more than one way to track Ajay down. He dialed Captain Reardon's office number. She answered on the first ring. "Morning, ma'am."

"Morning, Airman." The captain's voice was clipped and her words precise. He often thought she spoke the way a sniper fired. "What can I do for you?"

He imagined word of his early morning arrest had already made it to her ears.

"I'm trying to track someone down," he said, "and I'm hoping you could help. When I was in Afghanistan, I became friends with a local contractor named Ajay Joseph..."

"I can't say I remember him," she said briskly.

That didn't surprise him. There had been

hundreds of American servicemen and -women on the base, as well as hundreds of local contractors. She hadn't been wrong when she'd told investigators that he'd been a quiet man who kept to himself, though he seriously doubted she'd put the kind of negative spin on it that Preston had implied. A certain inner calm was important in the kind of Security Forces work that involved protecting high priority targets for long and potentially boring periods of time, when nothing was happening and there was empty desert spread in all directions. He hadn't socialized much with the broader team. Not because he hadn't liked them, but because he was the kind of guy who'd always preferred just having a couple of close friendships.

"He was an Afghan contractor who helped as a local liaison to get our weapons into the hands of the right people on the ground," he said, "and keep them out of the wrong ones. It's very important that I speak with him as soon as possible, but I haven't been able to reach him in weeks. I considered contacting your counterpart on the ground, Captain Teddy Dennis, but I don't know him personally and never served under him directly."

"May I ask what this is regarding?" Her

voice was guarded and cautious, even clipped. Under the circumstances, he wasn't surprised.

Lord, I hate asking anyone for help. But I don't have the resources to track Ajay down on my own.

"I need him to confirm a video communication we had on the morning of April 1," he said, knowing the date would probably trigger the same shudder of familiarity down her spine as it did his. "Ajay and I used to be in a small Bible study together, and consider each other friends. He had been dealing with a tricky situation and was looking for my advice."

Specifically, the young Afghan had been noticing some slight discrepancies in some of the weapons shipments and wondered if a fellow contractor was skimming off a few items to sell on the black market. Considering the desperate poverty some of his men were coming from, Ajay had been tempted to look the other way. But his new and growing Christian faith had been nudging him toward making a full report to Captain Dennis. He'd asked Chase to pray with him and had also promised to send through some supply records to get Chase's second opinion. He didn't want to ruin another man's life until he was positive theft was actually happening. The supply record emails had arrived encrypted. In the chaos of Boyd's breakout and the release of the K-9 dogs, Chase hadn't managed to unencrypt them before his laptop had been stolen from his truck. When Chase had gotten a new machine and asked Ajay to resend the files, Ajay had emailed back saying the matter had been resolved. It had been nothing but an accounting error. He'd also said that his father was ill, so he was going to visit his family in the mountains. Chase had wished his father a speedy recovery. That was the last Chase had heard from him.

He was thankful Captain Reardon hadn't pressed him for more information about the call. If Ajay had been right, and it had been nothing but an accounting error, he didn't want the notoriously aggressive Captain Dennis firing Ajay's crew over it.

"While we were talking, a phone call came in about the Red Rose Killer breaking onto base and releasing K-9 dogs," he said. "We'd been on the call from four fifteen onward, which proves I wasn't helping Boyd Sullivan on base that morning and was not involved in any of the crimes that took place. I got an email from him a few weeks ago telling me he was going to visit his family in the mountains and I haven't heard from him since. But, as you can imagine, I'm quite eager to talk to him now."

"While I don't recognize his name, Captain Dennis did recently mention his main liaison with one of the Afghan independent contractors had recently left," she said. "I assume we're talking about the same man. Communication lines in the mountains are virtually nonexistent."

"Did Captain Dennis have any idea when he'd be returning or how I could contact him?" Chase asked. "Do you know if Ajay's company has anyone who'd be heading up into the mountains who could try to pass along a message for me?"

He ran his hand over his face. Maybe he should have gone to Captain Dennis directly.

There was a heavy pause, which he knew meant Captain Reardon was choosing her words carefully. "Airman, I know you're frustrated. But you know that things don't work in Afghanistan the way they do here. It's the middle of the summer. The heat is extreme and we can't expect one of our partners on the ground to send someone wandering through a war zone to find one man who might not even remember a conversation he had with you three months ago."

He blew out a long breath. She was right

Captain Reardon or Captain Dennis would impact their careers, their work or their teams. Suspicion was like a toxin. It had been spreading through Canyon Air Force Base for weeks now, poisoning hearts and infecting relationships. He prayed that neither of the captains would face any trouble for helping him.

"Let me assure you that nobody you've served with believes for a moment you have anything to do with Boyd Sullivan," she added. "Hopefully, this will all be cleared up quickly. But, in my opinion, the best thing you can do right now is to lay low and let the investigators do their job."

"Thank you, ma'am, and thank you for the help. I really appreciate it."

"No problem, Airman."

They ended the call and he set the phone back in its cradle. Relaxing was the last thing on his mind. He'd been framed for murder, his life was falling apart and he wasn't about to sit around and wait for someone else to sort it. The uncharacteristic silence of his empty house surrounded him. He knelt in the mess and closed his eyes to pray. He couldn't remember the last time he'd been truly alone in his bungalow without his daughter and dog running around. He wasn't sure he liked it. Questions tumbled through his mind like

Ping-Pong balls in a dryer. His daughter's frightened face filled his mind.

Help me, God. I'm in really deep trouble and You're my only hope.

He opened his eyes and set out for Sunny Seeds Preschool.

"Doggy, Doggy, go find the phone!"

Maisy sat cross-legged on the brightly colored carpet in Sunny Seeds Preschool's large open classroom and chanted along with her students and classroom assistant, Esther Hall, as little Allie whispered the search command in Queenie's ear. Then Maisy let Queenie climb off her lap and into the circle. The children giggled as Queenie walked over to each one and sniffed them in turn. Then the small dog trotted off in the direction of the dress-up corner. Eleven small shining faces watched her go.

"Queenie finds phones!" Allie had explained to Maisy when they'd first gotten to the preschool. The toddler had then whispered something in the dog's ear and then Queenie had walked over and sat neatly in front of where Maisy's phone was on the table, and refused to move until Allie had patted her head. "I gave her a command just like Daddy. Queenie finds computers too."

Maisy hadn't even heard of an electronic-sniffing dog, let alone expected to find one in such a small and adorable size. All the K-9 dogs she'd met had been large, majestic and formidable breeds, like rottweilers, German shepherds and Doberman pinschers. But when Felicity and her newlywed husband, Westley, had dropped by with some dog food, she'd told Maisy that Chase and Queenie had done the electronic search of her home back in April and found two listening devices. Westley had then explained that while ESDs were relatively new in law enforcement, they had incredible abilities to sniff out the smallest electronic devices on command, as small as tiny thumb drives and picture storage cards, no matter where a criminal hid them. A beagle's small size and excellent nose made it the perfect breed for that kind of work. He said it seemed that while little Allie had been watching her father train Queenie at home she'd picked up how to give the dog the search command with the exact same tone of voice, intonation and gestures her father used. Ultimately, Chase would have to train the dog to ignore Allie's instructions. At least, thankfully, it only seemed to be Allie that the dog responded to that way.

Even then, Maisy had been a bit skeptical until Allie got Queenie to sniff out each arriving parent who came to drop off their child and then reported back whether or not they were carrying any electronic devices on their person. If they weren't carrying any, she moved on. If they were, she howled once, sat directly in front of their feet and stared.

She hadn't gotten it wrong once.

So now, on top of the general excitement of having a small dog as a very special visitor at the preschool, the regular circle time had turned into a game. Maisy, with Allie's help, held Queenie and theatrically covered the small dog's eyes while her assistant, Esther, helped one of the students hide the phone, and then Allie would give Queenie the command to find it.

The coat hooks, book nook and building blocks hadn't proven to be a challenge. This time Queenie sniffed around the costume trunk, then dove under the dress-up rack and disappeared in the costumes and uniforms for a second. Then her tiny furry head reappeared through the flowing fabric. She barked and sat. Maisy laughed. "Good dog."

She got up from the circle, went over and stroked the small dog's head. Queenie licked her fingers.

There was a short, polite rap on the glass

window separating the classroom from the front hallway. She glanced back. Her breath caught in her throat. There stood Chase, dressed in his crisp, clean uniform blues, looking every bit like a hero as he had the day she'd first laid eyes on him. Unexpected heat rose to her cheeks. Whether he was guilty or innocent of the crimes he was being suspected of, Chase's life was in serious danger. Her crushing on him like a schoolgirl was the last thing either of them needed.

Maisy broke his gaze and nodded toward where Allie now rolled on the carpet, giggling with Zoe's son, Freddy. The little girl hadn't noticed her father yet. Something softened in Chase's eyes as he glanced at his daughter, but he shook his head slightly and pointed to Maisy. Then he stepped back away from the window and out of sight. Seemed he wanted to talk to her alone for a moment before he greeted his daughter. She wasn't sure why, but once Allie caught sight of her daddy, Maisy suspected she wouldn't be in a hurry to let him go. Maisy wanted to talk to him alone too, more than she'd realized. She needed to look him straight in the eyes, ask him if he was guilty and demand the truth about why he had her father's cross.

Maisy turned back to the classroom. The

other preschool teacher, Bella Martinez, who taught the class next door, and her classroom assistant, Vance Jones, had taken their students outside to the playground. No doubt, her students would enjoy the opportunity to play with the other kids.

"That was fun, wasn't it?" she said, keeping her voice light and cheerful. "Now I think it's time for outside playtime. Everybody follow Miss Esther outside."

She waited and supervised, keeping a watchful eye as the slender and dark-haired newly qualified teacher led the herd of children out to the shady fenced playground behind the preschool. Two years younger than Maisy and very ambitious, Esther was the granddaughter of base commander Lieutenant General Nathan Hall and never tried to hide that she was eager to run her own class and not be anyone's assistant. But she was good with the students.

Maisy turned back to where she knew Chase would be waiting. She took a deep breath and prayed as she exhaled. *Lord, is this man guilty of the crimes he's been accused of? Help me be wise. Help me see the truth.* Then she raised her chin and pushed through the door into the small entranceway. "Hello,

Chase. Allie's outside in the back playground. It's fully fenced in and supervised."

Although, since paranoia and suspicion had spread across the base, a handful of the more overprotective parents had argued a locked five-foot-tall fence wasn't enough to protect their children from intruders. The preschool director, Imogene Wilson, had installed extra security cameras and keypad locks on the playground doors, but still some parents were demanding the school take down the beautiful and colorful picket fence that Maisy herself had painted and replace it with a much taller chain-link fence with barbed wire on top. One or two other parents wanted to cancel recess and field trips altogether. Thankfully, so far the preschool director hadn't given in.

Chase stepped back, nearly bumping into a cheerful hand-painted wooden sign of smiling fruit proclaiming Hugs Happen Here! He was so tall the top of her head barely came up to his chin, and not for the first time, she felt her eyes lingering on the strength of his arms and the breadth of his chest.

"Maisy, hi." His voice was oddly husky, as if there was something caught in his throat. Sad eyes searched her face, looking even more lost and alone than when he'd first walked into her preschool. "I… Honestly… Well…" Then Chase closed his mouth again and shook his head as his words failed him. If she'd ever seen someone in need of a hug, it was him. He swallowed hard. "How's Allie?"

"She's fine," she said, crossing her arms. "She was pretty confused and upset at first, as is to be expected. But she's a strong kid and very resilient. I let her take a pink hair bow out of the birthday box, which calmed her down a bit. She helped me make toaster waffles and fruit for breakfast and showed me how to get Queenie to hunt for cell phones."

He chuckled. "Did she now?"

"When Felicity and Westley brought over some dog food, Westley said to mention that before you integrate Queenie to the K-9 unit you'll have to train Queenie not to take commands from anyone else," she said, "including Allie. Although, he suspects Allie's only able to do it because she's done a really good job figuring out how to mimic you. She's a really smart kid."

His Adam's apple bobbed as if it stung to be reminded of his training with the K-9 unit that Westley had also told her was on hold while he was under suspicion.

"I don't know how to begin to thank you," he admitted. "Everything I can think of to say seems so inadequate considering what you did for us."

"How about giving me a straight and truthful answer? Did you have anything at all to do with the death of my father?"

He blinked as if something about her bluntness surprised him. But then he looked down at her again, his gaze strong and unflinching. "No, ma'am."

"Then how did my father's cross end up in your home?"

"I have no idea."

Her gut said he was telling the truth, but her brain was a whole different matter. She'd placed a lot of faith in the team investigating the Red Rose Killer in the past few months. The only thing that allowed her to sleep at night was the knowledge that some of the very best people she'd ever known were working around the clock to find Boyd and put him back behind bars where he belonged. But if Chase was innocent, then was her faith in the team misplaced? Or was she wrong to believe the man now standing in front of her?

Neither option was a comforting one.

"Did you ever have anything to do with Boyd Sullivan?" she pressed. Instinctively, her hand reached for his arm. She didn't know why. But somehow she found her fingers brushing the fabric of his uniform, as if trying to hold him in place. "Anything at all? Anything that could explain why the police think you would be helping him or hiding him in your home?"

Chase shook his head. Then he looked down at her hand like it had been a really long time since he'd seen a woman's fingers on his arm. His hand slid over hers, as if he was about to lead her into a party on his arm, or he was double-checking she was really there. The warmth of his touch spread through her skin. Then his clear and flawless eyes met hers again.

They were the same shade of green as a deep cool pond on a hot Texas summer day.

"No, ma'am," he said. "I give you my word. I would never put Allie in danger like that. She is my entire world."

She believed that, right? That no matter what else she knew or didn't know, Chase loved his little girl too much to sneak a man like Boyd Sullivan around the base and into their lives?

A chorus of panicked shouts erupted from the playground. Queenie barked and her students screamed. Maisy pushed through the door and pelted through the classroom and toward the back door, feeling Chase just one step behind her.

What was happening?

Then one child's voice rose above them all—"No! Stop! You're hurting me!"—and Maisy knew in an instant which student the voice belonged to.

It was Allie.

FOUR

Chase ran past her. She watched as his long legs sprinted through the classroom's maze of cushions, books and toys. He reached the door to the playground and yanked hard. His big hands struggled with the child safety lock.

"Wait, let me get it!" Maisy slid her slender body under the crook of his arm and in between him and the door. Her small hand brushed his large one out of the way. For a moment, his chest brushed against her back and her own fingers seemed to fumble with the same latch she'd done more times than she could count. Then it slid back and she slipped to the side as Chase yanked the door open and burst through.

"Allie? Allie!" His eyes scanned the fenced-in playground. Plastic toys, balls and trikes littered the ground. Bella was calling her students to line up against the wall for a head count. Bella's classroom assistant, Vance, was nowhere to be seen. Some of Maisy's students huddled around Esther. Others ran for Maisy, as she instinctively opened her arms to comfort them.

"Help me, Lord," Chase prayed aloud. "Help me find her!"

Maisy turned to Bella. "What happened?"

"I was getting my class to line up to come back inside when some kids started screaming about a stranger at the fence." Bella's dark eyes met Maisy's. The other teacher's face was pale. "I sent Vance to alert Imogene to initiate a lockdown and call police. Thankfully, all my students are accounted for."

But what about hers?

Maisy turned to Esther. "We have to get our class lined up and inside. Is anybody missing?"

"I don't know!" Esther's hand rose to her lips, suddenly looking years younger than twenty-three. She was breathing so fast she was almost hyperventilating. "It all happened so fast. Everyone was screaming. Kids were pointing at the fence. It was chaos." It still was. Esther gulped a breath. "I saw him. He was tall with a black hoodie and baseball cap. He had a bandanna over his face."

Like the figure she'd seen outside Chase and Allie's home. "Where?"

"I don't know. He ran, but I didn't see which direction." Esther's eyes grew wide. "Maisy, I think it was Boyd Sullivan."

It couldn't be! Could it? The world swam. A prayer for help moved through her. Bella's classroom assistant and the preschool director burst out the preschool back door and started helping a stunned Esther get students inside.

"Chase!" Maisy called. "There was someone at the fence! In a hoodie, hat and bandanna. Esther thinks it was Boyd Sullivan."

"Allie's gone." Chase spun toward her. Allie's bright pink bow was clutched in his hand. His eyes met hers, and it was like she could see through them to the pain piercing his chest. "I can't see her anywhere."

"We'll find her," she said, but he'd already run for the fence. His strong voice shouted his daughter's name.

She watched as Imogene helped Esther usher the last of her students through the door.

"Police have been called," Imogene told her. The gray-haired preschool director's face was grim. "Every teacher has their class on lockdown. All students were accounted for but one. Allie."

Maisy's gaze rose desperately to the fence that had given her such a false sense of security. *Oh, Lord, how can this be happening? How can a child disappear from my preschool in broad daylight? Had she been snatched over the fence?*

Maisy nodded numbly. She heard the sound of Bella locking her classroom door, the muffled children's cries from within the preschool and Chase's desperate calls for his daughter. Then one noise rose above it all—Queenie was howling.

"Let me go help Chase look for his daughter, Imogene, please," Maisy begged the preschool director. "I think I have an idea of how to find Allie."

Her boss paused. Maisy prayed the older woman would trust her on this. School policy was all hands on deck during a lockdown. But if Maisy could help Allie before it was too late…

"Okay," Imogene said. "I'll get someone to help Esther watch your class. When you come back, go to the front door and buzz in."

"Thank you."

The preschool director closed the classroom door and locked it behind her. Maisy ran for Chase.

"Chase, can Queenie track Allie?" Maisy asked. "I know that's not her K-9 specialty. But my grandmother used to say her beagle could find every one of her eight kids by just hearing their name. She said that breed had the best nose of any dog for finding her pack. And Allie's part of Queenie's pack. Right?"

Doubt flickered in Chase's gaze. He dropped to one knee. The tiny dog ran to him instantly. Her ears perked. Her unwavering brown eyes fixed on his face. He held out the pink bow.

"Queenie. Where's Allie?" His stern voice hid any hint of the doubt she'd seen on his face. "Go search. Go find Allie."

Queenie barked. Then the tiny dog pelted in a blur of brown, black and white fur toward the farthest corner of the fence. Chase matched her pace, scooping the dog up into his arms just steps before she reached the perimeter and held her to his chest as his long legs leaped over the fence. Then he set the dog down and they kept running over the grassy lot behind the preschool. Maisy cast one glance behind her at the closed door and then ran after Chase and the small dog.

Then she heard it, a faint voice sending hope surging through her veins. "Daddy! Help!"

"Allie!" Chase shouted his daughter's name and fresh strength seemed to course through him. "Hold on! Daddy's coming."

Maisy reached the top of the small hill and paused. The grass spread down to a parking lot below her. A slender figure, tall and shrouded in an oversize hoodie far too warm for the blazing sun was half carrying and half dragging a tiny squirming bundle of rage and fight toward the trunk of a car. Allie thrashed. Chase pelted toward his child, the dog howling at his heels. "Let. My. Daughter. Go!"

The black clad figure stopped, as if startled, turned back. Questions clashed hard and sudden, all within a fraction of a second, inside Maisy's frightened mind. If the person she'd seen had been trying to abduct Allie, why weren't they still struggling to get her into the car? Had everything happened more quickly than Maisy had realized? Had they hesitated? Or been unprepared and underestimated how hard it would be to make an upset toddler do anything they didn't want to?

"Daddy!" Allied wrenched her body from the kidnapper's grasp. She hit the pavement. Chase and Maisy kept running toward them. The figure fled, leaping into their vehicle and peeling off, without even stopping to close the trunk. Chase reached his daughter and scooped her up into his arms. He cradled her to his chest and kissed the top of her tiny blond head with such tenderness and fierce protection that Maisy felt tears rush to her eyes.

A fatherly love that deep had to be real, right? A man who loved his daughter that deeply just wouldn't invite a serial killer into his home. Would he?

Allie was babbling, something about a bad person and a picture, but her words seemed to run together in a stream of sounds. Then Allie's small tear-filled eyes met hers. "Maisy need hug too, Daddy."

Chase's eyes met hers in a split-second glance that seemed to last a lifetime. Then he nodded and slowly opened his arms for Maisy to take Allie. She reached out her arms and felt Chase slide the most precious thing in his world into her hands, just moments after coming within a hairbreadth of losing her.

"Thank you, Allie." She hugged the little girl close as her voice barely rose above a whisper. "You're right. I would really like a hug right now."

Chase closed his eyes and she watched as silent prayers poured from his lips.

"I get down now, Maisy," Allie said.

Maisy chuckled. She dropped to her knees on the soft ground.

"Are you okay?" She searched the toddler's tear-stained face. "Are you hurt?"

"No." The little girl shook her head. Her gaze dropped to the ground. "I bit, Maisy. I bit. I… I did bad…"

Tears filled her voice. *Oh, precious girl!* Maisy cuddled her closely.

"You're a good girl, you hear me?" Maisy said fiercely. "You did very good to bite the bad person trying to hurt you. You're right that we don't hurt or bite friends. But bad people aren't friends. You are important, Allie. Do you know what important means? It means you're special and I don't want to lose you. So if somebody bad hurts you, I want you to fight back and do whatever it takes to be safe, okay?"

Allie's eyes grew wide and Maisy's heart hurt having to tell her that.

"Because I'm im-por-tant," Allie said solemnly.

"Yes." Maisy hugged her. "Because you're important."

Allie took Maisy's face in her hands and made sure she was looking her in the eyes.

"Bad man hurt man, Maisy," Allie said.

Maisy rocked back on her heels and looked up at Chase. He looked as puzzled as she was. "Was the person who hurt you a bad man?"

Considering the slender build, Maisy had suspected it could be a woman.

Sirens rose in the air. Police were on their way. Within seconds, Security Forces would be surrounding her tiny preschool, followed almost immediately by parents and others as the news of what had happened would spread like wildfire through the base—especially if Esther stuck to her guns that the figure she'd seen was Boyd Sullivan.

"Bad man!" Allie said. Her voice rose with a tinge of panic. "Bad man hurt man!"

"She's been calling that out in her sleep," Chase said. He bent down and reached for Allie. "Come on, let's go."

The little girl's chin rose. "I wanna walk."

"Would it be okay if Daddy carried you?" Chase asked.

Allie shook her head stubbornly, sending her curls flying. Chase paused and Maisy could tell for a moment that he wanted to argue. She could only imagine how badly her father would've reacted if she'd insisted on walking instead of being carried at Allie's age after what had just happened. Allie's stubborn lip jutted out farther and quivered slightly.

"I wanna walk." Allie's voice shook. Her tiny hand grabbed Queenie's harness and squeezed it tightly. "Please, I walk with Queenie. Please, Daddy."

Maisy watched Chase's face, waiting and

half expecting him to sweep her up into his arms and carry the squirming toddler back over his shoulder as her father would've. Instead, he nodded. "Okay, Allie. If it's important to you, you can walk with Queenie. Maisy and I will walk right behind you."

Allie nodded. "Thank you."

Maisy felt an odd longing for something she'd never had move through her heart as father and daughter shared a look. Then Allie turned and led Queenie back toward Sunny Seeds. Chase and Maisy followed, walking side by side, two steps behind her. She watched as his long legs and large feet took tiny little steps to keep from catching up with his daughter.

"That was very kind of you," she said softly, "to let her take the lead like that."

"It seemed to matter to her and what matters to me is that she feels safe."

"Esther thought the man at the fence was Boyd Sullivan," she said. "But he seemed too slender to me. I would've guessed it was a woman, if Allie hadn't kept saying 'bad man.' Do you think it was the same person who was outside your house this morning?"

His back stiffened, as if every molecule suddenly drew itself to attention. "Who informed you of that?"

"Nobody informed me. I saw someone in the bushes outside your home in the early hours of the morning—"

"You what?" He stopped walking and turned toward her. His hand reached out, his fingertips coming within just an inch of brushing her shoulder. "When was this? What did you see? Why am I just hearing about this now?"

She stopped too and turned to face him. "This morning I was jogging near your home and saw a figure in the bushes." His mouth opened like he wanted to say something, but she didn't pause. "They were slender with a black hoodie, bandanna and baseball hat. I couldn't see their face and I couldn't tell if it was a man or a woman. I'm guessing they were about five foot eight or nine. Not that I'm the best at judging heights, but definitely taller than me and shorter than you. They drew a knife, I challenged them and they ran away. I then found some dried pink and purple pasta that I thought might've belonged to Allie's picture frame and turned it over to Captain Blackwood. I also made a full report."

His head shook. "Why didn't he tell me?"

"You'll have to ask him that yourself," she said. Allie was about five feet ahead of them now. Maisy started walking again. She was surprised and impressed that Queenie had the discipline to walk that slowly. "But I trust Justin and I know that whatever decisions he's making about this investigation he's doing it for the right reasons."

He matched her pace. "Why didn't you tell me?"

"Because we haven't exactly had much time to talk!" At the sound of her raised voice, Allie glanced back. Maisy smiled reassuringly. Allie smiled, turned back and continued walking. "We hardly had time to talk when you were being arrested, and I didn't want to say anything in front of Allie when she was already very upset. And then we'd barely been talking five minutes at Sunny Seeds before someone tried to abduct her."

His jaw clenched and she could see his facial muscles tighten under the skin. "I still don't understand how that could've happened. How could someone just show up at the back fence and kidnap a kid?"

It was a fair question, but it burned harsh in her ears. Did he have any idea how sick her stomach felt and how long the knowledge of how she'd failed one of her students so catastrophically would burn in her brain?

"I don't know," she said. "There were three

teachers outside. The area was fenced. The Texas Education Agency and the Department of Family and Protective Services recommended a student-teacher ratio of eleven to one—"

"I don't care what the guidelines are," he said tersely. "There is no excuse. It shouldn't have happened."

His voice was sharp, like she was a subordinate who'd messed up, or an airman whose mistake could've gotten people killed. Or like he was her father telling her yet again how disappointed he was in her.

"You're right," she said. "It shouldn't have happened."

He nodded curtly and turned to face the horizon. She watched as his spine straightened and a look filled his face, so determined and fierce that it made her breath catch. It was the kind of look that would have been as attractive and compelling as the sun itself in the eyes of a man who was her protector and defender. And downright terrifying in the face of an adversary.

Was it possible this man was as innocent as he'd seemed just minutes ago when he held his daughter in his arms? If so, why would anyone try to kidnap his daughter? Or be lurking outside his house? Or have planted her father's cross at his home, as he claimed?

The memory of her father's cross sitting in Justin's gloved hand filled her mind, unbidden.

Lord, am I foolish to believe he had nothing to do with my father's death? My father always said I wanted to bring home every stray dog and wild animal I spotted, not realizing my big old naive heart wouldn't stop them from hurting me. Is that what's happening here? Am I foolish for believing Chase's love for his daughter is so strong he'd never let the Red Rose Killer near her?

She turned back and was struck by his expression. It was a look that was silently asking her for something, like he was a desperately thirsty man and she had the only pitcher of cold water. And suddenly she realized what a foolish, narrow tightrope she was walking in her mind—not fully accepting he was innocent, but not believing he was guilty, either.

His footsteps stopped again and he swallowed hard as if making a decision he didn't want to make. "In light of everything that's happened, I think it's for the best if I keep Allie home, and she leaves your class and stops coming to Sunny Seeds."

* * *

Her blue eyes widened with such acute pain that for a moment he was tempted to take back his words. Instead, he planted his feet beneath him. Maisy didn't get what was happening here. How could she, when he barely got it himself? She seemed to have so much faith that Blackwood and the Security Forces would get to the bottom of everything. She'd trusted that her assistant teacher would keep a criminal from kidnapping his child.

She had a good heart, a better heart than anyone he knew, and he could tell that all she wanted to do was help. And yes, something inside him craved that, in a deeper way than he knew how to express. He wanted to feel like there was someone on his side. He wanted someone to make Allie smile and to hold his hand and tell him everything was going to be okay. But as much as he wanted to rely on Maisy like that, he couldn't. She was a sweet woman who meant well, but she deserved better than the mess and chaos he'd bring to her life.

"I'm sorry," she said. But this time her voice wasn't soft. Instead, it was firm. It was what he thought of as her "teacher voice," the one that demanded respect. "I'd obviously be sorry to see Allie leave my class, but you have to do what you feel is best for your child."

Lights danced ahead of them now, sirens blared loudly and Security Forces swarmed the preschool.

"You should've told me about the prowler outside my home earlier," he said, but even as the words left his mouth, he wasn't sure why he was bringing it up again. All he knew was there'd been a certain joy in his heart earlier as he'd jogged to Sunny Seeds. That joy was now gone.

Her chin rose. "I thought it was more important to ask why you had my dead father's cross in your possession."

Her words struck him in the chest and knocked him back an inch.

"Maisy!" a loud male voice called from within the chaos ahead. Preston was striding toward them.

"I've got to go," she said quickly. "If I don't see you later, Esther can help you gather up Allie's things." Then, before he could answer, she quickened her step until she reached Allie, leaned over and ruffled Allie's hair. "I'll see you later, Buttercup."

Then she ran toward Preston. Chase was about to follow when he felt a tiny hand brush his. "Pick me up, Daddy?"

"Of course, Sweet Pea." He bent down, swept her up into his arms and watched as Maisy disappeared into a sea of uniformed Security Forces officers.

He took Allie and Queenie home after making his statement to Justin Blackwood. The captain took his statement so professionally it was hard to imagine he'd been the same man who'd stood in the doorway while Preston had hammered Chase earlier. Then Justin questioned Allie gently, caringly even, letting her sit on Chase's lap while he softly tried to coax her side of the story from her stubborn lips. But all they'd gotten from Allie was a babbled mixture of words about "bad man" and "hurt man"—who Chase was beginning to think of as some character in a story he was never going to understand. They'd been left no closer to figuring out who had grabbed her or why the abductor had moved slowly enough that Chase had been able to catch up with them.

He didn't spot Maisy again before leaving, not that he didn't search her out in the crowd. He couldn't shake the feeling he'd been harder on her than he'd meant to be. Liz had often accused him of being unfeeling. It hadn't been true. It had been more like his feelings were locked somewhere inside a hidden heart, and he didn't know what to do about it.

He took Allie home, where the afternoon dragged out, long and endless, as he tried to juggle setting his home back to rights and replacing both the front door and Allie's window screen, while keeping her distracted and happy. To make matters worse, she was unusually fussy, wanting to stay close to him while he worked and bursting into tantrums whenever he tried to set up cartoons on his new laptop for her to watch.

That evening fell hot and deep, with a sun that seemed to grow redder as it sank into the sky. Sweat clung to his skin. Grime streaked his clothes. He dropped onto the couch.

"Daddy, I'm hungry." Allie crawled up onto his lap. "I need dinner."

He wasn't surprised. He'd made Allie her favorite peanut butter and banana sandwiches hours ago and she'd barely touched them. His eyes glanced at the clock. It was after nine. He should've put Allie to bed well over an hour ago, but every time he'd tried, she'd whined and clung to him, and he'd been too thankful just to have her there, alive and real and in his arms, to fight her. After all, it wasn't like either of them had anywhere to be in the morning. "What would you like for dinner, Sweet Pea?"

She looked up at him, sleepy and hopeful. "Carmen's pizza?"

He smiled at the cheekiness of the question. Carmen's Italian Restaurant was his favorite eatery on the base and somewhere he'd only taken Allie on very special occasions. They'd had someone there making balloon animals on her last birthday and they'd made Allie a hat with a bear on it. It seemed so very long ago. Would people stare at him now? Would they whisper among themselves as the man accused of helping Boyd Sullivan walked in the door? Would he ever feel comfortable sitting in a place like that again?

His stomach rumbled. On the other hand, Carmen's did a decent takeout. He could use a walk, and special pizza might help a terrible day end on a better note.

"How about we go for a walk to Carmen's and pick up pizza?" he suggested. "You could ride in the wagon? We could make it a special treat? Just for tonight?"

Her eyes grew wide. She nodded. "Queenie comes too. Queenie likes pizza."

"Right." He smiled. He wasn't sure Queenie had ever tried pizza. As a K-9 dog, her diet was supposed to be strict and limited. But he wouldn't have been surprised if Allie had been sneaking her all kinds of treats under the table when he hadn't been looking. "Good idea. If we walk, then Queenie can come too."

He loaded Allie up in the wagon with extra blankets for cushioning. Then he slipped the leash on Queenie and they stepped out into the night.

The evening surrounded them, warm and welcoming. Cicadas thrummed an invisible chorus from the trees. The thick scent of lavender and Texas lilacs filled the air, mingled with the smell of hot dogs and hamburgers from backyard barbecues. Laughter seemed to spill from behind every fence. It was like the whole base was out enjoying the July night. And he felt like an outcast or a phantom, moving through the shadows, with the rhythmic sound of the wagon wheels bumping over the evenly spaced cracks in the sidewalk like they were marching in lockstep with his feet.

The questions he'd been asked about Maisy's father filled his mind. He'd told Preston and Justin that Clint Lockwood was a hard man to train under. What he'd left out was that he'd appreciated that the Chief Master Sergeant was hard on him. There'd been something comforting about knowing there were standards and that those standards were high. When he'd marched in formation, he knew where he belonged and what needed to be done. He'd blended in, which was hard to do for someone of his height who'd gone through school as the tallest kid in his class. There'd been something about being in that uniform for the first time, and going through the same drills and exercises as every other new recruit, that made a person stop noticing the height, weight, age, gender or background of the person marching alongside him. Because they were a unit. A family. They were in it together. And he'd been just another part of that whole, doing his part and doing what needed to be done.

Liz had always questioned why he didn't strive harder to stand out and get more prestigious assignments. She hadn't understood. He'd always done the very best to serve his country, even on those days when all he was doing was directing traffic or guarding depots. But he'd never cared about being distinguished or important. He'd never minded less glamorous work. All that had mattered was being the best possible cog he could be, serving in whatever role he was assigned, in the amazing, glorious machine that was the United States Air Force.

His grandfather, despite his faults, had instilled that much in him—that it was better to quietly do your part to serve others than to claim fame and attention for oneself the way that Boyd Sullivan had. When Chase had been first deployed overseas, his grandfather had sent him a postcard. On it was a poem entitled "When I Consider How My Light is Spent" by John Milton, which ended with the reminder that standing and waiting was also a form of serving. That line had kept him focused on many long patrol nights. But what was he now? A random cog that had busted loose from the machine and fallen to the floor? A cog that the larger glorious machine was apparently willing to run without?

His eyes shot to the red-and-pink jet contrails crossing the sky and prayed for help without even knowing how to find the words.

"Look, it's Maisy!" Allie's voice made him stop. "Look, Daddy! It's Maisy! Hi, Maisy!"

He turned back. Allie was sitting up in her wagon, waving happily, but for a moment he couldn't figure out where she was looking. He crouched down to her level. "Where?"

"There! It's Maisy!" Her little hand pointed toward a fence to his right, with that odd laser-sharp focus that toddlers and K-9 dogs seemed to share. His eyes followed her gaze.

At first he saw nothing but indistinct figures in fatigues. Then the scene shifted and he caught a glimpse of a smiling blonde with a pixie haircut and peach sundress.

"See, Daddy?" Allie asked, her eyes serious with the clarity of innocence. "Can we go say hi?"

"No, honey, Miss Maisy is busy with friends," he said as the glimpse of Maisy's smile sent unexpected feelings through his chest. He looked away. One of his shoelaces was hanging long. He knelt and tied it sharply, pulling on the laces so tightly he could feel the pinch at the top of his foot. He'd been curt with Maisy and had brought danger to the door of her preschool. Regret washed over him with a million words he wished that he could say.

He wondered what his life would've been like if he'd had the courage to speak to her when he was a much younger man. If he hadn't become romantically involved with Liz. If he'd waited instead to earn Clint Lockwood's approval to date his daughter. He wondered what it would be like to be the man standing beside Maisy, protecting her from harm, instead of being suspected of aiding the man who'd ripped her father from her life.

A hand landed heavily on his shoulder, its

grasp firm. A low and deep warning growl sounded to his right. Then he heard a voice, male and with unrelenting authority. “Stop right there. Don’t move.”

FIVE

Chase turned slowly and looked up at the tall and muscular form of dark-haired Technical Sergeant Linc Colson. His huge attack-trained rottweiler, Star, stood alert by Linc's side. Instinctively, Chase felt his body stand to attention. He saluted. "Evening, Sergeant."

"Evening, Airman." Linc returned the salute. Suspicious eyes glanced down at Allie and Queenie, and then scanned Chase's face. Chase found himself oddly impressed that the sergeant didn't drop his guard because Chase was with his daughter. "Care to tell me what you're doing crouching behind the fence outside my new home?"

"It wasn't intentional," he said. He clasped his hands behind his back. "I was out walking with Allie and she was excited to spot her preschool teacher, Maisy Lockwood, through the fence. I stopped and laced up my boot."

It was the truth and he said it without a

flicker of a muscle on his face. But that didn't seem to damper the wary look in Linc's eyes. Was this how it was going to be from now on? Would he never be able to so much as stop and tie his boot without rousing suspicion? Chase met his gaze and held it firm like a man who had nothing to hide.

"Hi, Star!" Allie chirped. He looked down. Despite the fact that his presence lurking at the other side of the fence had set Star growling protectively, the dog's tail was now wagging. Allie waved her hand happily at the huge dog, keeping her fingers just far enough away from the canine's fur to let Chase know that his instruction to never touch a dog without permission had sunk in. "Daddy, Star is Freddy's new dog!" Allie said cheerfully. Then she pointed at Linc. "That's Freddy's new daddy."

The two men paused. Allie's bright eyes looked from Linc to Chase. She pointed to each man in turn with that tone of voice he knew meant she was trying to be helpful. "You're Freddy's daddy and you're my daddy! You're both daddies!"

She said the word *daddy* with both a force and an innocence that made an emotion catch in his throat. She said it like *daddy* was a special word and like she expected everything should be all right between him and Linc because they were both daddies. And the fact that the word meant something so important to her small, innocent mind filled his heart with thanksgiving.

He prayed he'd never give her any reason to think any other way.

"Linc, is everything okay?" An unfamiliar woman's voice dragged his attention to the fence. While he didn't know the voice, he definitely recognized the face of the woman now opening the side gate and stepping through. Zoe Sullivan, a petite woman with flowing brown hair, was a flight instructor and Boyd Sullivan's estranged half sister. She was also the single mother of a three-year-old boy named Freddy from Allie's school. As Zoe reached for Linc, he saw a tasteful gold band on her left hand, and the final pieces of the puzzle clicked into place. Looked like she was Zoe Colson now. He'd vaguely heard the single mother had recently gotten married and moved into a new house with her husband. But he'd never been much for standing around gossiping, let alone reading the anonymous blog that some mysterious person at Canyon had set up to spread rumors about the Red Rose Killer's crimes, his possible accomplices and the state of the investigation.

At least now he understood better why Linc was so protective of his home and wary of anyone lurking outside. He wondered how it was for them, always wondering where her half brother was, who he'd target next and how soon he'd be caught.

"Hello, Sergeant." Chase saluted her. "Sorry to cause a disruption to your evening. I was just passing by. Congratulations on your recent nuptials."

"Thank you." She smiled and returned the salute, but she also looked slightly confused. He suddenly wondered if anyone said nuptials anymore. "It's Chase, right? You're Allie's dad?"

"Yes, ma'am."

Through the open gate now he could see the small audience walking toward them, men and women he knew, at least to say hi to, and who now no doubt wondered if he was guilty of the crimes he'd been accused of. There was Westley and Felicity James, and Westley's canine partner, a German shepherd named Dakota. Also, a red-haired search-and-rescue dog handler he vaguely recognized as Ava Esposito with her Labrador retriever, Roscoe. And his friend Isaac Goddard, who he'd done basic training with, with his own golden retriever named Tango. Only Maisy stood alone on the porch with a plate of food in her hand, and her friends standing between them like a shield.

"Allie!" Freddy tore across the yard like an enthusiastic missile. "Hi, Allie! I have hot dogs! You want hot dogs too?"

"Actually, we should get going," Chase said. He reached for the handle of the wagon. "I promised Allie pizza tonight. I'm sorry to interrupt you. I hope you have a wonderful evening."

"Daddy," Allie whimpered softly. "Don't want pizza. Want hot dogs with Freddy."

"Actually, Chase, can we talk? If you have a moment?" Maisy called out to him. She started down the porch steps, crossed the backyard and looked around at her friends. "If it's okay with you guys, there's something I need to talk to Chase about and I'd like to do it tonight, if that's possible."

In other words, she wanted to talk to him, somewhere where they weren't alone and she had her trusted friends close.

Zoe and Linc exchanged a look that spoke the kind of volumes that only couples who'd been through a lot and understood each other deeply shared. Then Zoe said, "We do have plenty of food, if you'd like to stay for a hot dog."

"Absolutely." Linc stretched out his hand toward the backyard. "Freddy has been really eager to show somebody his new tent."

"Thank you," Chase said, once again finding the words inadequate for everything going through his mind. He reached his hand toward Allie to help her out of the wagon, but she was already scrambling toward Zoe's outstretched hand. Taking Allie in one hand and Freddy in the other, Zoe walked the little children over to where a long table sat overflowing with hot dogs, burgers, veggies and salad. Felicity pulled Maisy aside and the two women exchanged a quiet word. A warning, perhaps? He wouldn't blame Maisy's friends for telling her to be cautious around him. If anything, he was thankful to know she had people watching her back.

Westley stepped forward. Chase saluted. "Sergeant."

Westley returned the salute. "Good to see you and Queenie. How has training been going?"

Chase searched the master sergeant's face. The look in his eyes was cautious, much as Chase would have expected in his position, but not hostile. He appreciated that. If he were in Westley's shoes, he'd have felt the same. Just a few short weeks ago, these people had been his new colleagues in a team he'd just begun to feel like he was a part of. Now, he was just thankful they were still giving him the time of day and hadn't already decided on his guilt, like Preston had.

"Not bad," Chase said honestly. "Not as good as I'd have liked or of the level that would've been expected if I'd been able to continue training Queenie with the team. But we've been doing some basic drills at home every day."

Westley nodded. "Good to hear it. The more consistency you're able to instill, the easier time Queenie will have reintegrating with the team."

Chase could only hope that he and Queenie would still be partners when that happened and that lingering suspicion—or, worse yet, charges being filed for crimes he'd never even dreamed of committing—wouldn't mean she was assigned to someone else.

"Why don't you unleash her and let her socialize?" Westley added. "Being around the other dogs will help with her reintegration too."

It was a good idea. He bent down and unclipped Queenie from her lead. Her nose nuzzled his hand. Her huge brown eyes looked up into his, then, tail wagging, she ran off after the other dogs. He stopped and watched as his small dog disappeared into a cluster of bigger canines, feeling oddly like a father sending his child off to play. Then his eyes ran over to where Allie and Freddy were happily piling plates with food under Zoe's watchful eye.

Had he been too hasty to pull Allie from Sunny Seeds? Would she miss the other kids? All he wanted was to protect her.

"How is she doing?" Maisy's soft voice seemed to brush over the back of his neck like a cool breeze.

He turned toward her and realized that Westley had stepped back to join Linc by the barbecue, leaving them alone.

"It hasn't been the easiest afternoon," he admitted. "But, hey, she's a strong kid. How was the rest of your day? I'm really glad to see your friends have your back."

"My afternoon was probably about as hard as one could be. Security Forces stayed at Sunny Seeds all day. Most parents came to pick up their kids early, and they all had a lot of questions about what had happened. But being out with friends tonight helps." Maisy glanced back over her shoulder to the people now gathered around the back porch and yard, all of whom seemed to be doing an excellent job of watching them without actually letting it look like they were watching. Did any of them believe he was innocent? Did some of them think that by bringing him in closer they'd trip him up and find evidence?

"We've all become a lot closer, in a way, since Boyd broke out of jail and..." She left thc sentence unfinished as a deep sadness filled the depths of her eyes. *And killed several people, including her own father.* She blinked back tears. "It brought some of us together in a tighter knit family. But all across the base I see it tearing other people and relationships apart. The fear. The suspicion. The way people have stopped saying howdy to strangers and started giving each other the stink eye. It's like Boyd doesn't have to be literally on base killing people for him to cause destruction."

Yeah, he knew what she meant. Even if he didn't know how to explain it himself.

"I don't know how to put this into words," he said. "But it's like Allie has somehow grown younger since the morning Boyd Sullivan broke onto base. She cries more. She babbles and has more tantrums, not to mention more nightmares about 'hurt man' and 'bad man.' There was a lot of mess to clean up in the house today and she was pretty agitated." He twisted Queenie's leash, wrapping it around his hand like a fighter preparing for a bout against an unknown enemy. "There are moments when she's so grown up she's like a little girl. Then other times, when she's upset, it's almost like she's still a baby."

"I know exactly what you mean," Maisy said. He felt her hand brush his sleeve. Her bright blue eyes met his, so dark in the center and filled with far more compassion and understanding than he had any right to hope to see. "She's dealing with a lot. But she's resilient. She'll bounce back. Playing with Freddy tonight should help. We just all need to hold on until life gets back to normal." Something caught in her throat as she said the word *normal*.

Suddenly, he found himself turning toward her and taking both of her hands in his.

"Look, I'm sorry about what I said earlier," he told her. "I owe you an apology. I didn't mean to make it sound like I thought Sunny Seeds was unsafe or that Allie would be better off without you. I was frustrated. I was worried. My daughter had just been grabbed and almost abducted. I saw the Security Forces surrounding Sunny Seeds, and I was worried that I was bringing danger into your life. But I know there's no place better for Allie than Sunny Seeds, and nobody better for her to be spending time with than you. I just don't know who I can trust anymore."

"You can trust Justin Blackwood." Her hands squeezed his tightly. "My father liked him, a lot."

He wanted to believe his investigation was in the hands of someone trustworthy and honest, who'd follow the evidence all the way to the end and until it cleared his name. "But how well do you know him?"

"Better than I know you."

She watched as he rocked back on his heels. What had he expected? That she was on his side? That she would somehow be his ally? No, she was on the side of the truth. She wanted her father's killer to be stopped. She just wanted justice to be done.

Chase still hadn't spoken. She felt her mind fill with the memory of Preston leaning over her shoulder as she sat at her desk at Sunny Seeds and pulled up the security footage.

"The so-called kidnapper was probably a girlfriend or his ex-wife," Preston had said. "A man like Chase uses women. Just like he used you today."

"Hey, Maisy! We've got Frank! He's live!" At the sound of Ava's voice calling from the patio, she turned. Ava, Isaac, Linc, Zoe,

Westley and Felicity were all gathered around a laptop set up on the middle of the picnic table. Ava waved her over.

Maisy turned back to Chase. "I'm sorry, one of our friends serving in Afghanistan has a birthday today. So we thought we'd set up a group call."

"Frank Golosky?" he asked. A slight and tired smile crossed his lips.

"Yes," she said. "Do you know him?"

"We were in the same Bible study when I served overseas. He's a really great guy. One of the best."

Chase was right. Frank was a really good man. More important, he was someone whose opinion Maisy trusted. What was Frank's opinion of Chase? she wondered.

"He's great," she said. "We were hoping his brother, Drew, would join us tonight. But apparently he's on leave for a few days and didn't return Zoe's calls. He's not exactly that reliable."

Linc was holding the laptop up high as if trying to find a spot where everyone could see Frank's laid-back grin and he could see everyone. She scanned the yard. Allie and Freddy were sitting in the pop-up tent, eating hot dogs and potato chips.

"Why don't you come say hi to him?" she

suggested. "I'm sure he'd be happy to see you." And she'd get to see what Frank thought of Chase.

She turned and walked over to the group, tugging on his arm slightly to get Chase to follow her. Happy small talk surrounded the group, although she got the impression that Frank was somewhere between amused and frustrated that his brother, Drew, hadn't shown. Then Frank's eyes met hers through the screen. "Hey, Maisy! Glad to see you made this shindig too. How's life been treating you?"

There was a softness in Frank's voice when he asked the question, and it was a tone she was so used to. Some days it felt like everyone had collectively decided that from now on she'd be treated like she was fragile and delicate. People rarely came out and openly asked about her actual grief. No, that was a hidden thing, like the bloody cross under the floorboards of Chase's home that nobody dared pry out. Instead, they tap danced above her pain, in a kind, gentle and loving way, as if they were afraid of hurting her.

Except Chase. He didn't talk to her like a victim. He actually told her what he thought. Maybe because he knew what it was like to be on the outside too.

"I'm good," she told Frank. "There's someone else here who says he knows you."

She waved Chase forward. Frank's wide beaming smile told her everything she'd wanted to know.

"Well, my man McLear! How are you, buddy?" Frank chuckled, leaning forward.

Chase set Queenie's leash down on the porch railing and raised a hand in greeting. "Hey, Golosky! Happy birthday! It's good to see you."

"It's good to see you too!" Frank leaned back, crossed his arms and nodded to the other people around her. "This guy here led the best Bible studies. Bar none. He'd spend hours researching and planning them. Whenever I showed up and he was in charge, I knew we'd be in for some heavy-duty thinking. How's it going, man?"

An awkward pause spread through the group gathered in the backyard, as if everyone was collectively holding their breath to see what he'd say.

"Not great, to be honest," Chase said. "Though it could always be worse. I can fill you in more another time, on a private chat. But quickly, have you seen Ajay Joseph recently? It would really help if I could talk to him."

Frank's smile dimmed. "Nah, I haven't. Sorry, man. I heard his father was sick, so he went home to his village to be with his family."

Chase blew out a long breath. "That's what I heard too."

A happy bark sounded through the video call.

"Beacon!" Isaac leaned forward, a smile exploding across his face as a beautiful gold-and-black German shepherd leaped into view.

"Yeah." Frank ran his hand over the dog's shaggy fur. "I figured you'd want to see him."

Conversation around the patio shifted to talk about how the dog was doing. Beacon had been partnered with a close friend of Isaac's who'd died in a plane crash in Afghanistan and had recently been lured back to base by one of his former unit members. From what Maisy could gather the dog's retraining wasn't going well. Chase stepped back down the porch steps and disappeared into the darkness behind her. She couldn't tell if it was because he was disappointed about not being able to reach his buddy Ajay or if something about hearing the other K-9 officers talk about Beacon's retraining bothered him. Either way, she felt herself turning and following him down the porch steps, as if joined by an invisible thread.

She trailed him down the yard, away from her friends and the safety of the porch light, past the tent, where Chase popped his head in quickly to wave at Allie, and then through the happy mass of barking dogs and wagging tails, where Maisy lowered her hands to feel the soft noses greet her as she went. Finally, he reached a thick log at the very end of the yard, against the backyard fence, its wood worn as if people had been using it to sit and think for ages.

Chase settled down onto the log, propped his elbows up on his long legs and dropped his head into his hands. His shoulders rolled forward, as if his back was on the verge of collapsing under an invisible weight, and something about it wrenched at her heart in a way that she didn't know how to put into words. Then he looked up. His eyes met hers. The gentle yellow glow of a streetlight on the sidewalk behind the fence fell over the strong lines of his jaw. Sadness washed over his features. She sat down beside him and suddenly she found herself blurting out the one thing she'd wanted to tell someone but hadn't known how.

"I'm tired of people asking me if I'm okay,"

she said. "I'm not okay. I haven't been okay in a long time. I don't know when I'm ever going to feel okay again. My father is dead, Chase. Some horrible person murdered him."

And you're accused of helping him...

He ran his hand over his head.

"I'm sorry," he said. "I shouldn't have interrupted your party. I don't belong here."

"I asked you to join us," she pointed out. "Because we need to talk."

About so many different things, she didn't know where to start. She hated how they'd left things at Sunny Seeds. She wanted to tell him about what she'd seen on the security footage. She wanted to yell at him about how he could possibly be so clueless about how her father's cross had ended up in his home, and admit that she didn't know whether or not to believe him. She also wanted to hug him, even though she wasn't sure why and was pretty sure she shouldn't.

"I know you deserve an explanation," he said. Raw emotion pushed through his voice. "For all of this. But I don't have one."

"I saw the security footage, Chase," she said. "It was too grainy to make out the face of Allie's kidnapper. But they were definitely after her. They lurked there for a while, as other kids came by the fence. There were easier targets. But they waited to grab her."

He ran his hand over his face as if trying to wipe the image from his mind. "They wanted my child. Specifically, my child."

Preston's warning that Chase knew Allie's abductor clattered in her mind.

"Preston Flannigan told me that statistically you knew whoever kidnapped Allie," she said. "That it was likely her mother or someone you're in a romantic relationship with—"

"Her mother gave up the rights to her the day the DNA test proved she was my child!" Chase's jaw tightened. "I don't have any romantic relationships. And I don't much care what Preston Flannigan thinks of me."

Something dark flashed in his eyes, warning her to drop it. But how could she?

"Who's Ajay Joseph?" she pressed. "Why is it so important you talk to him?"

"He's my alibi for the morning Boyd Sullivan broke out of jail and sneaked onto base," Chase said. "He's an Afghan local who was working as a contractor over there. He was a middleman between the United States Air Force and a group of locals on the ground who we were helping supply weapons and aid to. We were friends. We studied the Bible together and he was very new in his Christian faith. We'd talk sometimes after I moved back, and he'd call for advice. He called for advice shortly after four in the morning on April 1 because—and I need you to keep this between you and me—he'd noticed a few things missing from a warehouse manifest and suspected one of the locals might be selling things on the black market. We talked until I got the call that the Red Rose Killer was on base, that people had been killed and dogs were loose. It was pandemonium."

She felt her face pale. Yes, she remembered.

"We hadn't heard about your father at that point," he said. "But it was all hands on deck. I got off the phone and found my daughter was already up, and Ajay had ended the call. I'm guessing the sound of the dogs barking, the phone call and the chaos on base woke her up. I strapped her into a backpack carrier, put the leash on Queenie and we went out and helped round up dogs. Later, I emailed to apologize for cutting him off so suddenly and he emailed some encrypted files I promised to look at. He didn't want to wreck some guy's life without proof. The next email I got from him told me that he was going to visit his family in the mountains for a while. I figured he wanted a break away from base to think and pray."

"But you still have his files and a video log of the call," she said.

"My laptop was stolen from my truck shortly afterward," he said. "Whoever did it also got my gym bag full of dirty clothes and my toolbox—so everything needed to frame me of a crime."

But it still didn't explain her father's cross. She didn't answer and he didn't say anything more. Instead, they just sat there, side by side, their shoulders barely an inch away from touching, and their breaths rising and falling in rhythm together. He turned to her and she felt her breath tighten in her chest under the weight of the unspoken words in his eyes.

What was wrong with her? How could she be so attracted to a man who'd been accused of something so terrible? How could she crave the safety of being inside the strong arms of a man who, if not guilty, was at least being targeted by criminals? Yvette, the base nutritionist, had told her once that there was an eighty-to-twenty ratio of men to women on the base.

Why was this one man the only one to ever tug at her heartstrings this way?

Crush was such a silly, childish word to

describe a full-grown and independent woman's feelings for a man. Yet, as she felt the heaviness of the emotions she'd never act on weighing down on her heart and suffocating her breath from her chest, she couldn't think of a better word for it.

"Maisy?" Chase said softly. His fingers brushed the back of her hand, like he wanted to take it but wasn't about to let himself do it. "I'm sorry for all of this. You deserve so much better than what I'm putting you through right now, and I wish..." His voice suddenly faded, leaving the thought unfinished. He swallowed hard. Then he sat back. "Never mind."

She grabbed his hand and squeezed it, even as he tried to pull it away. "Tell me. Please, Chase. What do you wish?"

The electronic chime of a cell phone alert sounded so close behind them it was like it was coming from the fence itself. Chase dropped her hand. They jumped to their feet, coming eye to eye with a dark figure in a hoodie and bandanna on the other side of the fence.

"Stop!" Chase said. "Right there!"

The figure turned and fled.

SIX

"Stay here!" Chase ordered. "Get Allie inside. Keep her safe!"

Then he ran down the yard, back toward the gate. He whistled sharply. Within a second, the small beagle was by his side. Man and dog burst through the gate. It clattered behind them.

Maisy turned, a prayer on her lips, and ran back to the house. She'd barely taken five steps before Ava, Westley, Linc and Isaac rushed up to her. Felicity was standing on the porch. She didn't see Zoe or the children.

"Maisy!" Linc said. "What happened?"

"Someone was spying on us over the back fence. Chase went after them. Where's Allie?"

"In the house with Zoe and Freddy," Linc said. "Description of the suspect?"

"Slender. Black hoodie. Black hat. Bandanna over the lower half of their face. Taller than me, but shorter than Chase. Like I said, Chase and Queenie ran after them."

"And you saw this person yourself?" Ava pressed. "Firsthand?"

"Absolutely."

The airmen exchanged a quick and pointed look. Then they gathered their dogs, with a series of whistles and calls, like a quickly mobilized team. Linc called to Felicity to brief Zoe. Westley scooped Queenie's leash up from the porch, held it under Dakota's nose and told her to track. The German shepherd barked, ran down to the end of the yard, then back through the gate, with the other dogs and trainers steps behind. Maisy stood there a moment and watched the empty space where they'd been. Then she turned back to the porch where Felicity still stood. Maisy walked toward her.

"You're sure Allie's in the house?" Maisy asked. "I promised Chase I'd make sure she was okay."

"They're in the kitchen washing their hands," Felicity said. There was an odd look on her face. It was like there was a wild coyote standing behind Maisy and she didn't know how to warn her without spooking it. "They're decorating cupcakes. Freddy's really happy to have a friend over and I think Zoe's happy to be able to reach out and be there for Allie. She, better than anyone, knows what it's like to live under a veil of suspicion."

Her tone implied that she wasn't so sure the rest of their friends had been as happy to have Chase around.

Maisy looked in the window. Zoe was standing at the kitchen table now. Maisy watched as Zoe helped each child in turn climb up onto a chair and then spread brightly colored candies, tubes of icing and sprinkles in front of them. Maisy reached for the back door, but before her fingers could brush the handle Felicity pointed to a chair. "Sit. Please. We need to talk."

Felicity sat down. Maisy turned her eyes away from the happy domestic scene inside the kitchen and sat beside her.

"About what?" Maisy asked. She could hear barking and yelling in the distance, and prayed they'd catch the prowler.

"About the handsome man you've been making eyes at tonight," Felicity said.

Maisy felt heat rise to her face.

"Allie is one of my students," she said. "She's like this bright little light in my day and I care about what happens to her."

"And her father, Chase?" Felicity asked.

Maisy looked down at the wooden porch

slats beneath her feet and shrugged. "I honestly don't know what to say."

"But you like him," her friend said gently.

"I do." Maisy nodded, miserably. "I think I have for a long time. But it was just an innocent crush, you know? It's not like I thought anything was ever going to happen between us. I just enjoyed seeing him for that few moments a day, when he dropped Allie off or picked her up. I liked that little bit of a lift, a happy little jolt, it gave to my day. It sounds foolish."

"Not foolish. Human," Felicity said softly. "It took me a while to warm up to Westley because I wasn't sure he liked me. I had no idea at the time he was fighting feelings for me. But he was my commanding officer, so he couldn't act on those feelings. Once he became my protector and I finally let my guard down…my heart took over."

Maisy watched as she spun her new wedding band around on her finger.

"All I'm saying is I care about you, you're my friend and I want you to be careful," Felicity added. "Everyone on base is under a lot of stress and it's making everything seem more important and urgent. Just look at Westley and me, or Zoe and Linc. You've never served in the military or been deployed, but there are moments in this career where it's like everything's sped up and we've all stepped on a moving sidewalk without realizing it. It's scary, and exciting, but it also leads to people making bad decisions."

"I'm not making any decisions," Maisy said. "All I did was agree to watch Allie for a bit this morning and have a conversation with Chase about the case."

"I know," Felicity said. If possible, her voice was even more gentle than it had been before. "And I'm not saying you did anything wrong. But I've seen the way you look at him and Chase isn't just the father of one of your students. He's been accused of killing your father."

"And you think I don't know that?" Maisy's eyes rose to meet Felicity's. Then her head shook. "I'm sorry. I just can't bring myself to think he's guilty."

Felicity nodded, like she was hearing something much deeper than what Maisy was saying. "And maybe he's not. I'm keeping an open mind about him and I don't know what Westley thinks. But whatever this thing is that's drawing you to him, I think it's a lot deeper than you want to admit. Just promise me you're going to keep yourself safe."

Maisy pressed her lips together and nodded. She didn't know what to say. Felicity had gotten her dead to rights. She liked Chase, in a very simple, real and honest way. There was just something about him and little Allie that got to her, no matter how much she knew that the smartest and safest thing for her to do was steer clear.

Chase stopped in his tracks and looked around in all directions. The night was still around him. The base's perimeter fence spread out ahead of him. The figure he'd been chasing was gone. He felt Queenie by his side. "I don't know what happened, Pup. They were here just a minute ago."

Help me, Lord, what do I do now?

The night had set in deeper and darker while he'd been talking with Maisy. Now, black Texas skies spread dark above his head, filled with the kind of huge bright stars he'd grown up believing a man couldn't find anywhere else.

He looked down, his eyes adjusting to the dim light, and saw the dog's attentive face turned to toward his, ready to search if only he said the word.

But track what? She wasn't trained to track people, only electronic devices. Would that work? He was pretty sure the figure had been carrying a cell phone, judging by the phone alert sound he'd heard. Normally, he'd never think to give Queenie the command to go search out in the world without knowing exactly what she was looking for.

But desperate times…

He turned to her and instantly felt his small partner snap to attention. "Queenie, go search!"

Instantly, her nose went to the ground. He watched for a second as she sniffed, back and forth, methodically. Then she howled and disappeared from view. Okay, so where had his dog gone? He'd trained her not to run away and to stay within his line of sight. He kicked himself for having not gone back for his leash before running after the hooded figure, but it hadn't felt like there was time. He grabbed his phone from his pocket and scanned the fence. Then he saw it, a gap barely more than a few inches under the fence, leading out into the thick woods behind the base. He bent down and shone his light through the chain-link. Sure enough, there was Queenie, sitting on the other side, with her head cocked as if she was wondering what was taking him so long.

All right, then. He ducked low and realized the only way he was getting through the fence was on his stomach in a combat crawl.

He crawled through and came out in the thick ravine surrounding the base. Queenie ran up to him and then away again a few steps with another little howl.

"I'm coming!" he said. Queenie tilted her head to the side. "Go search!"

She took off running, her little body moving easily through the deep scrub and underbrush. He ran after her. For a moment, nothing filled his ears but the rustling sound of Queenie crashing through the trees, his own footsteps pelting after her and the panting of their breaths.

Then he heard voices yelling behind him, the sound of dogs barking, and realized he was being pursued. Someone was chasing after him. Just like that, he'd gone from the hunter to the hunted, running like a fugitive in the night. Too late, he remembered Captain Justin Blackwood's warning not to leave the base without informing his office. He stopped and turned around. His hands raised instinctively. Light flashed in his face, blinding his view, just in time to see the German shepherd barreling toward him. Its teeth were bared. Its powerful lungs barked and a chorus of dogs joined in behind it.

"Dakota, heel!" Westley's authoritative voice sounded in the darkness. Instantly, the dog stopped, turned and trotted back to his partner. Chase raised his hand to his eyes and shielded his facc from the light as slowly the group came into view.

Westley, Linc, Isaac, Ava and their canines were striding through the woods toward him, with a purpose and strength that reminded him of the Air Force K-9 poster that had hung over his too-short bed as a child.

"Airman Chase McLear?" Westley called.

"Sergeant!" Instinctively, Chase felt himself salute. The lights dropped from his face. The cops exchanged a look. "There was a figure in a hoodie and bandanna spying on the house. Queenie and I ran after them and chased them into the woods."

Despite the fact that he and these cops had been standing around casually in a backyard less than an hour ago, he was now standing up at full attention. He was a suspect—he could see it in Westley's eyes—and he would never have their trust until his name was cleared.

If it was cleared.

Linc crossed his arms. "Outside the base perimeter?"

"We were following the suspect and they slid under the fence."

"You saw them go through a hole in the perimeter fence?" Ava asked, probing deeper.

Chase planted his heels beneath him and reminded himself their questions weren't personal. They'd been searching for Boyd Sullivan for months. The existence of a hole in the perimeter big enough that he could squeeze through no doubt rattled them.

"Queenie found the hole in the fence, actually," he admitted. "I didn't see it. When I lost sight of the suspect, I remembered I'd heard what I thought was a cell phone message alert. So I told Queenie to track the cell phone."

He felt the familiar press of warmth against his calf. He looked down. Queenie was back by his side. Had she given up because he was no longer following? Had she lost the scent? Or had she returned because he was in trouble? She was such a good dog. His heart ached to know her K-9 training was on hold because of him.

A pause spread through the group, as if each of them was weighing internally what to say.

Then Westley turned to the others. "My suggestion would be that Linc gets back to the house, checks in on his family and the others and calls it in if they haven't already. Make sure Security Forces know about the hole in the fence. Ava, can you and Roscoe search the woods and see if you can come up with any trail of the person that Chase saw?"

"Absolutely." She nodded.

"I'll go with her," Isaac said quickly. "No one should be roaming around out here alone in the dark."

Ava smiled, grateful.

"Agreed." Westley said. "I'll stay out here and talk with Chase for a bit."

Linc and Star disappeared through the night in one direction, while Ava and Roscoe, and Isaac and Tango disappeared in the other. Westley nodded to Queenie. "I take it she lost the scent?"

Chase nodded. "I'm guessing so."

"You left this behind at the party." Westley reached out and handed Chase Queenie's leash. He guessed that's what Dakota had used to track him. "It's ill-advised to have a dog tracking without her leash on in an unknown outdoor setting. It's different when it's a contained or known environment, and I know as an electronic-sniffing dog, the vast majority of the searches she's done have been indoors. But, generally speaking, unless you've got an attack dog chasing down a suspect, when you're in the ravine, we keep leashes on. Now, let's see if she can still track that cell phone."

Westley had been the lead K-9 trainer on base, until recently when Master Sergeant Caleb Streeter had taken over day-to-day operations due to the Red Rose Killer's threats on Felicity's life. Chase knew the man had the experience and the skill to direct this search.

Chase took the leash and clipped it onto Queenie's harness and told her to search. This time she trotted into the woods, leading Chase at a brisk pace. He followed, feeling Westley and Dakota one step behind him. Queenie reached a pond, dark and gloomy in the night. She whined and sat down. Had the figure tossed their phone in the pond or swum through it to hide their scent? Either way, the scent was gone. Chase leaned down and ran his hand over the dog's head.

"It's okay, girl," he said, softly. "You did a really great job."

He reached into his pocket, pulled out a piece of dried sweet potato and gave it to her.

When he turned back, Westley was watching him with a curious look on his face. "What did you just give her?"

"Sweet potato," Chase said. He watched as Queenie chewed her treat, then handed one to Westley. "I did some research about her breed. Beagles aren't picky eaters but they are prone to weight gain if they eat too much, and

I can't always keep track of everything Allie drops on the floor, so I switched to dried fruit and vegetables as her main treat."

Westley rocked back on his heels, looked at Chase for a long moment and then nodded slowly as if answering a question in his own mind. Then he handed the treat to Dakota, who took it eagerly from his hand. They turned and started walking back toward the fence.

"Isaac got a bit of bad news when he was talking to Frank," Westley said. "As I'm sure you know, Isaac's best friend, Jake Burke, died in a plane crash in Afghanistan that almost took Isaac's life as well. Beacon was Jake's K-9 partner. The way Isaac tells it, Beacon and Isaac helped keep each other alive until rescue came. But according to Frank, Beacon is responding badly to his new trainer. He's aggressive. He's paranoid. If the situation doesn't change, Beacon might have to retire."

He blew out a long breath, and Chase could see just how heavily the situation was weighing on him. They kept walking.

"I've got to tell you," Westley said, after a long moment, "it can be very hard on a dog to change partners. Sometimes they get aggressive. Sometimes they get confused. Some dogs are flexible and are able to adapt easier than others. But some dogs are simply untrainable when they lose their human partners."

They reached the fence and walked along it until they found a checkpoint gate. They showed their identifications and walked through. Chase made a mental note to call Justin Blackwood's office later and report what had happened, before he was questioned yet again on how his identification had been used to sign into the base when he hadn't signed out. They walked for a few more minutes until they reached the soft yellow illumination of Canyon's residential streetlights. Chase could also feel Westley's eyes on the sweet, gentle, attentive and intelligent dog now trotting by his side. It felt like he was getting an unexpected evaluation in his and Queenie's training. A huge and unspoken question seemed to move through the night between them, and Chase was thankful when Westley came out and addressed it.

"How long has it been since you were put on suspension and Queenie stopped formal training with the K-9 team?" Westley asked.

"Three weeks and four days," Chase said. He took a deep breath. "Do people on the K-9 team really think I had anything to do with the Red Rose Killer's escape, the lost and injured dogs and the murders on base?"

"I couldn't tell you what people think—"

"What do you think?"

Westley stopped and turned toward him. His eyes met Chase's unflinching and guileless gaze. "I'm doing my best to keep an open mind."

Chase guessed that was all he could ask for. They turned to start walking again. But there was one more question Chase had inside him, one that he wasn't sure he had the courage to ask.

"If this investigation into these false accusations against me continues to drag on, how long do you think I'll be allowed to stay inside the K-9 training program before they reassign Queenie to a new partner?"

"I don't honestly know," Westley said. "That's no longer my call. Sergeant Streeter is now in command and running the K-9 training center on a day-to-day basis. I'm checking in regularly as needed, but I wasn't in on his decision to allow you to continue training Queenie at home when you were suspended. Although the fact that he did makes me think he didn't expect the investigation into you to last this long."

Well, that's something at least, Chase thought.

They turned onto Linc and Zoe's street.

"I won't sugarcoat it," Westley added. "Like I said, it can be very hard on a dog to change trainers, and Queenie has been out of training much longer than I would've liked. My guess is that Caleb definitely won't let the situation go past the end of July and into August."

Chase blew out a hard breath. So twelve days, then.

"But honestly?" Westley stopped outside Linc and Zoe's front gate. "If it were up to me, I wouldn't let it go on that long. This situation has stretched out much further than it should've. I'll be filling him in on what happened tonight and telling him that in my opinion, if you're not cleared and reinstated back on active duty by the end of the week, Queenie should be reassigned to a new partner and trainer."

SEVEN

Allie's small head of blond curls snuggled tightly into Maisy's side as they curled up beside each other on Zoe's couch. In front of them, little Freddy lay on his stomach on the brightly colored carpet, watching one of his favorite DVDs of Sunday school songs and bedtime stories flicker on the television screen. He had one arm thrown around his father's massive rottweiler partner, Star. There was something about seeing the huge dog cuddled up beside the small boy that filled her heart with both a surge of happiness for Zoe and Freddy having found Linc and a longing to one day feel that safe and protected.

Behind her, in the other room, she could hear Felicity, Zoe and Linc talking in hushed tones, outside of Freddy's earshot. She wasn't sure what to think of the fact that Linc and Star had come back alone, or that Linc had asked if she'd mind watching the children while the three of them talked. Which was okay by her. After all, the three of them were members of the United States Air Force who had signed up to serve their country and were part of the Red Rose Killer investigation. All the adults who'd been at the barbecue tonight had been, and while her friends had always done their best to include her in conversations about their hunt for the Red Rose Killer, as much as they were able to tell her, it didn't change the fact that she would always be a civilian and a preschool teacher.

Being left to watch the children had never been a role that bothered Maisy. It was something she'd always gravitated to. Growing up, she'd gone to so many military get-togethers and parties, and watched the men and women in uniform stand around talking about important issues. They all seemed so strong and confident, statuesque and bold, the best that the country had to offer, standing there holding plates of food and having dizzyingly complex conversations that made her head spin. She'd watch how other young people her age—most of whom were already in the Civil Air Patrol cadet program—would stand around the edges of adult conversations, joining in and listening keenly, and it was as if she could see their minds growing into the men and women they'd be one day.

But that wasn't who she was. That just wasn't her world. Sure, she'd stood by her father's side for a while, but then she'd invariably found herself slipping off to the room where the little children and babies were. She'd played with the infants and started little games for the toddlers and preschoolers, making them smile and laugh and freeing up their tired parents to go socialize with the other adults. She'd liked it there. She fit there and felt like she belonged.

Just like she seemed to fit here, comfortably on the couch with Allie McLear snuggled into her side and Freddy lying happily at their feet. Allie's eyes closed. Then the little girl drifted off into a comfortable sleep. Maisy sighed. There was something about just having the little girl near that filled her heart with joy. Allie was like a little bundle of...well, of everything. She was so full of energy, happiness, curiosity and joy.

If what Chase said was true, first her own mother had abandoned her and then her father had been accused of being the accomplice of a serial killer. Maisy's heart ached. That was far more than any child should have to bear. How much more would she have to go through? Maisy cradled her closer into her side. She prayed that whatever came next, Allie wouldn't have to face it alone.

She heard voices rise in the kitchen, as if the volume of the conversation had been turned up a notch by the arrival of someone else, not that she could make out the words. Then she felt fingers brush her shoulder and heard the sound of the deep and strong voice she'd have known anywhere. "Maisy?"

She turned her head, careful not to jostle a sleeping Allie. Chase was standing behind her. His hand pressed gently on her shoulder, as if silently nudging her to stay seated.

"I'm going to try to let her sleep," he said softly. "She hasn't slept through the night in ages and she's always overtired. If I'm careful, I might be able to carry her home and put her back to bed without her waking up."

She nodded. Freddy turned his curious little face up toward them, quizzically looking up at them over Star's back. She raised a finger to her lips and hushed him softly. "Allie's asleep."

He nodded and turned the television volume down three notches. She smiled. He was such a good kid, and she was both happy and thankful to see how well the little boy had adjusted to having Linc in his life. She gently nudged the sleeping girl deeper into her arms, then stood, feeling Allie's head fall against her chest. It was only then that she realized Chase's shirt and jeans were streaked with dirt, like he'd been crawling across the ground.

"You might want to clean yourself up a bit," she said.

"It's okay. I brought a blanket from her wagon." He draped the soft pink-and-purple blanket over his shoulder and chest. She walked around the couch to him and gently slid Allie into his arms. Her hands brushed against his forearms as she did so, and for one fleeting moment, she felt the strength of his biceps beneath her fingertips. She stepped back and watched as a sleeping Allie snuggled happily against her father. An odd and almost unnameable longing surged inside her chest, to know what it was like to feel that safe. But she didn't know if it was that she wished she'd known growing up what it was like for her own dad to care for her that way, or if she longed to know what it was like as a woman to be held safely by such a man.

"What happened?" She kept her voice low, hoping the sound of the television would still protect Freddy's young ears. "Did you find them?"

But she knew from the look in his eyes,

even before he shook his head, that the answer was no.

"They got away," he said. "Queenie tracked them to a hole in the perimeter fence and we followed the scent out into the woods. Ava and her dog, Roscoe, are still searching the ravine. Isaac and Tango went with them."

Yeah, no one should be alone in the woods right now. The fact that they'd found another hole in the fence filled her with dread. That Boyd Sullivan was able to sneak onto the base was a horrible, daily, pressing reminder that even inside a guarded perimeter, no one was ever truly safe.

"We have Security Forces patrolling the perimeter," he said, as if reading her thoughts. "The hole will be fixed tonight."

But what about the next hole and the next? How had this horror, this fear, this tragedy continued on so long, with no end in sight?

"Well, I reckon I should be saying goodnight," Chase said.

She nodded. "Yeah, you should probably get Allie home to bed before she wakes."

But still, he didn't move and neither did she. They just stood there, with their eyes locked on each other, and Allie sleeping softly on her father's chest.

"Goodbye, Maisy," Chase said.

She bit her lip. "Good night, Chase."

He turned and walked toward the kitchen, passing through quickly and professionally, with a quick word to the others, a nod of his head and Queenie by his side.

She waited five minutes after he'd left and then walked into the kitchen and joined the others. Their serious conversation had changed to small talk by the time she made it in there. On purpose or by design, she wasn't sure. But she was thankful for it. She hung around just long enough for Ava, Isaac and their dogs to return, sadly with no trace of the person that she and Chase had seen.

Her goodbyes were quick despite the fact that all of her friends had collectively decided to walk her to her car. There were kind smiles and deep hugs, along with the promises that people would be praying for each other and the reassurances that Boyd Sullivan would be caught soon. They were the kind of comfortable words that she'd gotten so used to both hearing and saying that they'd become part of the regular patter around the base. And while they meant a lot, something in her heart longed for the day conversations like these would be a distant memory.

She dreamed of her father that night. It wasn't the first time he'd walked into her dreams since his death, leaving her with disjointed thoughts she wasn't sure what to make of or how to understand. In this dream, he'd been promoted to General Lockwood and was in full dress uniform, white and gleaming with dark shoes of shining polished leather. She was a teenager in the dream, barely more than sixteen, she guessed. They were walking through a lavish fruit market filled with exotic fruits of all shapes and colors that she was sure didn't exist in the reality of the waking world. She'd asked her father if she was allowed to go out on a date with Chase, who somehow she knew was a teenager himself.

Every good tree bears good fruit, her father told her in the dream. *Chase isn't bearing good fruit. Trees that don't produce good fruit should be cut down and burned in the fire. Jesus said that.*

She'd argued back with him that Jesus had also said that trees should be given an opportunity to grow first. Jesus had specifically said that a tree should be tended, cared for and loved for a while before the farmer would truly know if it was ever going to bear fruit.

Then she'd woken up before her father could answer. She sat up and blinked, her eyes still swimming from sleep. The clock read seven in the morning. It wasn't possible.

How had she slept through her alarm? For the first time since her father's death, she'd missed her morning run, and now she had less than an hour to shower, dress, eat and make it to Sunny Seeds to open the door.

It was only then she realized her cell phone was ringing and wondered if that was what had woken her. She swung her legs over the side of the bed, grabbed her phone off the bedside table and stood. It was Oliver Davison, the highly focused FBI agent who was off the base chasing down leads on the Boyd Sullivan investigation. Why was he calling her? Fear stabbed her heart so quickly that her fingers fumbled, dropping her phone on the soft white carpet before quickly snatching it up again.

"Hi," she said, feeling her breath catch in her throat. "It's Maisy."

"Good morning, Maisy," Oliver said, his voice held both dedication and sadness, along with a weariness that hinted of a long career filled with such calls. "I'm calling as a courtesy to let you know that while Security Forces were searching the forest and ravine around the Canyon Air Force Base perimeter, the body of a man was found. We've identified him as Airman Drew Golosky—"

Her intake of breath was so sharp he paused.

"Do you know him?" he asked.

"I know his brother, Frank," she said. She sat down on the edge of her bed, grabbed a handful of blankets and squeezed tightly. "Last night I was with a group of people who placed a video call to Frank in Afghanistan yesterday. Drew was invited to the barbecue, but we hadn't thought anything of the fact that he wasn't there because he was on leave."

She'd never imagined he was dead.

"A red rose and a note were found under his arm," Oliver continued. "We believe it was the work of the Red Rose Killer. His uniform was missing, and his identification was used to enter the base within the past few days..."

Her head swam, and for a moment, the FBI agent's words seemed to distort and blur into white noise. Boyd Sullivan had been on the base in the past few days? He'd just strolled right through the gate with a stolen uniform and ID? If Boyd Sullivan was the "bad man" Allie was frightened of, did that make Drew Golosky the "hurt man"? But how would little Allie have seen them? Besides, Chase had said Allie had been yelling about a "bad man" for months, not that she had any proof of that.

Oh, Lord, please save us from this nightmare.

Dread washed through her veins, the feeling both sickening and familiar. How many more of these phone calls would there be? How many more people would die?

"Who else was in attendance at the barbecue yesterday?" Oliver asked.

She ran through the names, realizing as she did so that it was very unlikely she was the FBI agent's first call to someone who'd been at the barbecue, and so she might be telling him information he already knew. She wondered how many identical conversations he'd been through so far today and how many more he had to go. Her eyes closed.

Oh, Lord, I feel trapped inside a nightmare with no sign day is ever going to break again. How many voices have called out to You to guide investigators to find and capture Boyd and his accomplice? Please, may Your answer come soon.

She hoped that when that day came, Chase and little Allie wouldn't be caught in the trap.

"I want to assure you that we're doing everything in our power to catch your father's killer and make sure he's brought to justice," Oliver said. "We will catch him, Maisy. I give you my word. In the meantime, please don't let your guard down."

At least the Security Forces had the courtesy to knock on his door this time, instead of breaking it down and throwing a warrant in his face, Chase thought, as he stood there in his PT uniform and looked through the front door of his bungalow at the two investigators standing on his front step. After he'd made the impulse decision to follow Queenie through the hole in the fence after the hooded figure, he shouldn't have been surprised to have Captain Justin Blackwood and Lieutenant Preston Flannigan appearing at his door. Allie was still asleep, and when he'd lost track of Queenie in the few minutes between feeding her breakfast and making coffee, he'd figured that she'd sneaked into the little girl's room. But before he could even open his mouth, Queenie had run to his side.

He saluted. "Good morning, sirs."

The officers returned the salute.

"At ease," Justin said. "May we come in?"

Well, that was definitely a change from door breaching. Not that he was about to let his guard down. Last night's barbecue had been an all too painful reminder that he was a suspect and would always be a suspect no matter how nicely or politely people treated him.

Chase's eyes rose to the clock. It was ten after seven.

"Absolutely," Chase said. "But if we can

keep the volume down, I would appreciate it. My daughter is still asleep. She normally wakes up around now for preschool, but I decided to let her sleep in this morning. She's been sleeping really badly."

After last night, he was feeling even more conflicted about his decision to keep her home from Sunny Seeds. Had he made the right call? Would Allie be better off with life being as normal as possible and spending time with other kids? How much of his decision-making process was being influenced by his own conflicted feelings about Maisy? Something about seeing her last night and that moment they'd shared on the bench had shaken the fragments of his broken heart. And that same feeling had been there just as strong after he'd gone chasing after the fugitive and come back to pick up Allie.

He let the police into his living room, where they stood around his battered wood dining room table, stained from endless painting, coloring and crafting he'd done there with his daughter. "Would you like to sit down?"

"Thank you," Justin said, and Chase couldn't help but notice that this time the captain was doing the talking, while Preston stood silent one step behind him. The men sat, with Chase and Justin opposite each other and Preston at the end of the table. Justin pulled an envelope from a folder under his arm and even before reaching inside, Chase knew without a doubt that it contained the picture of another body. "We regret to inform you that another body has been found. The remains of Airman Drew Golosky were found in the ravine by search teams in the early hours of the morning. We believe he is one of Boyd Sullivan's victims."

The picture lay on the table in front of him. The tall, strong airman had been stripped of his uniform. The remains of a rose were displayed on the body along with a note. Poor Frank. Chase's head dropped into his hands as a heavy weight sank like a stone to the bottom of his stomach. The fact that his friend's brother had died hit him far deeper than the fact that these men were no doubt here to question him as a suspect.

God, please be with Frank right now and his entire family. Comfort them. Surround them with Your mercy. Uphold them with Your mighty arms.

Queenie's head fell on the top of his foot as she lay down beside him. He reached down and brushed his fingers over the top of her head.

Justin pulled a notepad from his pocket and flipped to a new page.

"We believe Airman Golosky has been dead for seven days," Justin said. "His identification and uniform were used by Boyd Sullivan to get onto base twice during this time." Which lined up perfectly with when someone had reported seeing him at Chase's house. "I need to ask you if you can account for your whereabouts on Thursday, July 12, Friday, July 13 and Monday, July 16."

Chase paused for a long moment before answering, as he searched his brain for anything abnormal about his regular schedule on those days.

"Each day followed the same routine," he said finally. "I took Allie to Sunny Seeds at oh eight hundred. Then I came home and trained Queenie around the house until sixteen hundred. I then took Queenie to pick Allie up from preschool and we spent the rest of the afternoon and evening together."

Justin jotted down a few notes. Chase noticed he kept the book shielded, so neither he nor Preston could read it. "Any witnesses to corroborate your story?"

"No, sir," Chase said. "Just my daughter."

Who was hardly a reliable witness. How had he never noticed just how small and lonely his life had become? That there'd be no friends or colleagues there for him, showing up with meals or inviting him for dinner to help him through these difficult and trying days. Was Liz right? Did he push people away?

Just like he'd pushed away Maisy.

"How well did you know Airman Drew Golosky?" Justin asked.

"Well enough to say hello," Chase said. "I couldn't say the last time I'd seen him or we'd spoken. His brother, Frank, and I served together in Afghanistan and I consider him a friend."

"And when was the last time you spoke to Frank Golosky?" Justin asked.

"Last night," Chase said. "I was at a barbecue at the home of Sergeants Linc and Zoe Colson. It was Frank's birthday."

Justin's composure flickered slightly, but it was only a moment before his features returned to their neutral position. "Are there any witnesses to your conversation with Frank Golosky last night?"

"Absolutely," Chase said. He listed every name, rank and title of the people who had been at the barbecue, taking note of how Preston's nostrils flared when he mentioned Maisy's name.

"And what did you discuss?" Justin asked.

"We exchanged pleasantries and I asked him if he'd seen Ajay Joseph recently," Chase said. "He had not."

"Could you please give an account of your entire evening last night? From the beginning."

He did so, starting with being spotted by Linc outside the fence and then moving back to the video call with Frank. "Then I had a brief conversation with Maisy Lockwood—"

"What was the nature of the conversation?" Preston interjected. It was the first question he'd asked and he did so with such force that Chase was surprised he didn't actually bang his fist on the table.

"We discussed the kidnap attempt on my daughter at Sunny Seeds," he said. "She asked why I'd been looking to speak to Ajay Joseph, and I told her that he was my alibi for the morning of Sunday, April 1. I also assured her I had nothing to do with Boyd Sullivan's crimes and her father's death." But there'd been more to the conversation than that. Something deeper. Something he'd felt when her hands had brushed against his. "Then we heard what sounded like a cell phone alert and turned to see a figure in a hoodie and baseball cap on the other side of the fence, with a bandanna covering the lower half of their face—a figure who I must stress matched the description of the person who tried to abduct my daughter yesterday and was also seen lurking outside my home. Queenie and I gave chase."

He then explained in detail everything that had happened next, from reaching the fencc, to making the call to go through, to being joined by the other K-9 officers and dogs, to Queenie losing the scent. He would go over it all, every word, in slow, laborious detail, leaving nothing out. It was the only way he'd clear his name, by cooperating and behaving like a man who had nothing to hide.

Preston sat silently through the rest of the talk as Justin went over every single question and detail that the lieutenant had drilled him on in their last interrogation, including new ones about what had happened the day before. But while Preston had questioned him like an angry dog trying to chase a rat into a corner, Justin's questioning was calmer, quieter and more methodical. Instead, it was like Chase's entire life was a tower of wooden blocks, and Justin was slowly poking and pulling each one, trying to see if he could pry it loose and make Chase's whole world crumble and fall. Preston's aggressive assault Chase could stand against. Justin's slow dismantling of his life shook him far more.

Allie cried out softly in her sleep and he could tell without even glancing down under the table that Queenie had gone from lying down to sitting up in response. His little girl wasn't fully awake yet, but she wouldn't sleep much longer.

"I have something to show you," Justin said. He pulled a folded piece of paper from his pocket. "I received an emailed response from Captain Teddy Dennis serving in Afghanistan. I had reached out to him in regards to your communication with Ajay Joseph. He mentioned that your former supervisor, Captain Reardon, had reached out to him as well."

He breathed a sigh of thanks that Captain Reardon had done as she'd said and that Teddy had responded.

"What did he say?" Chase asked, forcing himself not to ask all the other questions tumbling through his mind. Had he been able to reach Ajay? Had Ajay confirmed his alibi? If so, why was he still being questioned?

"You can read it for yourself." Justin slid the paper across the table with a grim look that made any hope Chase might've been tempted to feel dissipate before it could even form. He stared at the paper for a moment. Then he unfolded it and read.

It was an email sent from the official address of Captain Teddy Dennis, three lines long, blunt and to the point. Yes, he could confirm that somebody by the name of Ajay Joseph had been the liaison between the United States Air Force and an independent Afghan contractor and had coordinated with Chase McLear personally. The email went on to say that Mr. Joseph had gone home to visit his family in the mountains in early April, had resigned from his role in late May and that Teddy was unaware of whether he was returning to work or how to contact him. The captain closed the letter by saying that Captain Blackwood shouldn't hesitate to contact him again if he could be of any more assistance.

"Disappointing," Chase said. He looked down at the letter for a long moment. Then he refolded it and slid it back across the table. "But Captain Reardon did say she'd look into whether the records of my video calls with Ajay could be recovered. Maybe she'll turn something up."

"What did you discuss during your last conversation with Ajay Joseph?" Justin asked. His eyes rose to meet Chase's and there was a new look in there that Chase couldn't decipher. It was piercing.

"No, sir." Chase folded his arms on the table. "I'm sorry, but I promised to keep everything he said in strictest confidence."

If he had been able to receive, decrypt and read the files Ajay had sent, he could've had actionable data to report. Ajay had known that Chase wouldn't have been able to keep silent if he'd seen actual evidence of theft or fraud. But as it was, all he had were rumors, ones that could ruin innocent people's lives.

"What was the nature of the conversation?" Justin pressed.

"Again, it was personal, sir," he said. "And nothing that has any bearing on this discussion."

"Don't you think that's for me to judge?" Justin demanded. "Do you understand what's happening here, Airman? You've been accused of being an accomplice to multiple crimes, including murder. You've been accused of aiding and abetting a serial killer. Your career is hanging by a very thin thread, and you're dangerously close to being in handcuffs. To be very blunt, the only thing I care about is the truth. If the truth is that you're innocent, then I want that sorted out and settled as quickly as possible so that I stop wasting my time and start chasing other leads. If you're guilty, and your silence allows Boyd Sullivan to hurt a single other human being, then you should have no doubt that you will be caught and punished to the full extent of the law. So the quicker you stop being coy and start getting real with me, the faster a killer will be off the streets and the easier life will be for your daughter."

Chase sat back in his chair. It was the longest string of words he'd ever heard come out of Justin's mouth and he could tell by the way the usual smirk had faded from Preston's face that it surprised him too.

"So, I will ask you again, Airman, what was the nature of your conversation with Ajay Joseph? Why did he call you that morning? What did you discuss?" Justin asked.

Chase felt his shoulders straighten. "With all due respect, I'm not trying to obstruct justice, sir. I simply believe what I discussed with him is irrelevant."

Justin leaned forward. His eyes narrowed like a searchlight, locking Chase in their focus. “Even if it gets people killed, lands you in jail and destroys your daughter’s life? Are you really that heartless?”

EIGHT

Heartless? The single word smacked Chase with a ferocity that stole the breath from his lungs and made a fire flare inside his veins and threaten to consume him. He hadn't wanted to tell them that Ajay had called about suspected theft in his team, because Ajay's last email had told him it'd been nothing but an accounting error and Chase wasn't about to blurt out that a friend had suspected one of his men of stealing from the United States Air Force. Trust was everything in a war zone. Even the suspicion of theft could cost countless impoverished Afghan locals their livelihoods. He'd seen independent local contractors fired for less. And Justin thought that meant he didn't care about his daughter? That he didn't care that Boyd Sullivan was out in the world murdering good men, like his friend's brother?

The captain had no idea how hard Chase

fought day after day to withstand the barrage of questions, accusations, suspicion and dirty looks, or how much inner strength it took him not to stand up, flip the table over and shout his innocence at the top of his lungs.

"I don't want to hurt Ajay!" Chase felt his voice rise. "He's my friend. He's new in his faith. He's dealing with a family crisis. I'm not about to throw anybody under the bus to save my own life."

Preston groaned. Yeah, he didn't expect Preston to get it. But was he mistaken, or had something actually softened behind Justin's eyes?

Chase took a breath. He would tell them the truth. But nothing specific that could damage Ajay or the men who'd worked for him.

"My grandfather was Senior Master Sergeant Donald McLear," Chase went on. His voice dropped. "He told me a good man never repeated slander and that even when there was proof, a wise man knew when to hold his tongue. Ajay was concerned that someone he knew might've committed a nonviolent crime. It turned out the allegations were false and I'm certainly not going to repeat them. He asked me for my advice on the matter and I agreed to look at his evidence. But his evidence was on my missing laptop and I never had the opportunity to look at it. Ajay later emailed that he'd been wrong, no crime had occurred and it had all been a mistake. All I know is that my friend Ajay was doing his best in a difficult situation and I have no desire to make his life more complicated or ruin a potentially innocent stranger's life, just to save my own skin." He crossed his arms and leaned back. "I know all too well how being stitched up feels."

He realized as he'd said the words that he could've probably said that much earlier and found himself wondering, for the first time, if his reluctance to trust other people was making his life even more difficult than it needed to be. But opening up and trusting people had never come easily to him. He felt protective of Ajay, who'd confided in him. The last thing he wanted was to find out Captain Dennis was breathing down the local contractors' necks because of him.

His grandfather always warned him that any word he spoke and any weakness he showed could be weaponized against him. Surely, it was best to stay a closed book. Life was safest if he didn't let anyone in.

Silence fell around the table. Justin leaned back and let out a long breath. "And you're sure that's the only person you're protecting?"

"Bad man hurt man! No!" A plaintive cry came down the hall, shattering the moment of tension and stealing any answer Chase might've given. Allie's gentle whimpering turned into a full on cry. Instantly, Chase pushed his chair back and stood, forgetting for a moment where he was and who he was with.

Justin and Preston stood too.

"I think we're good for now," Justin said. "Don't leave the base without going through a main checkpoint again and informing my office, under any circumstances, or I will be forced to reexamine whether further restrictions should be placed on your movement. If you can think of anything that could be helpful, don't hesitate to give me a call." He laid his business card down on the table. Allie's cries grew louder. "We can see ourselves out. Go tend to your daughter."

"Thank you, sir." Chase saluted and the two men returned the salute.

He left the men in his living room and half strode, half jogged down the hallway to Allie's room. She was sitting up in bed, damp blond curls plastered against her sweaty face. She reached for him.

"Bad man hurt man, Daddy," she said.

"I know, Sweet Pea," he said. *Not that I*

know what you mean by that. He swept her up into his arms and held her tightly. His fingertips gently brushed her hair back from her face. “Daddy’s here now. You’re safe.”

A gentle tongue licked his arm tentatively. He glanced down. Queenie had jumped up on Allie’s bed and was standing there, her tail wagging gently, as if she knew something was wrong and wanted to help. Chase closed his eyes and hugged his daughter closer, feeling her tiny fists tighten around the fabric of his T-shirt.

Please, help me, Father God. I love Allie so much. She’s my whole world. Save me from the snare I’m in, for her sake. I don’t want to even let myself think of what will happen to her if I don’t get out of this mess.

“Put me down, Daddy,” Allie said, after a long moment. “I need to go to school now.”

He opened his eyes and eased her back to arm’s length. Her chin still quivered, but her eyes blazed with a stubborn determination that he knew meant that she was done crying for now. He hoped that she never lost her fortitude and resilience.

“What would you think of staying home from Sunny Seeds with me and Queenie today?” he asked.

The jut of her lower lip told him the answer even before her words did.

"No, Daddy. I need to go to school. I need to go see Maisy."

Of course she did. He set her down and she wriggled from his grasp.

"I dress myself." Her little chin rose and she pointed to the door. He almost smiled. Seemed she was feeling independent today. Hopefully that was a good sign.

"All right, then, I'll go get your breakfast ready." He stepped back. It had been two months since she'd decided she needed to get dressed all by herself. After watching her futilely but stubbornly wrestle with the wooden dresser drawers, refusing to accept his help, he'd put all of Allie's favorite clothes in a special set of pink and purple plastic drawers at toddler height on a shelf by the wall. "I'll be right outside if you need me, okay?"

Or if she tried to put her red knit Christmas dress on again in the middle of a hot Texas summer.

"Bye-bye now, Daddy!" She waved, with that determined gesture that meant she expected him to leave. Her face was so serious he had to battle the urge to laugh. That old cliché that she'd grow up fast had seemed so far away when she was a tiny baby, crying in the night for her missing mother. Now he felt like he was realizing for the first time just how true it was. He stepped back into the hallway and waited a second to see if Queenie would be ordered out along with him. Then he closed the door three quarters of the way when he realized that apparently the dog was allowed to stay.

His heart ached to think of what would happen the day he'd have to tell Allie that Queenie was leaving. The deadline Westley had given him nipped like a wolf at his heels.

Lord, please. Help me. Rescue me from that day.

He turned and only then realized that Preston was still standing in his living room. Chase's shoulders set. He turned and strode back into the room. "Can I help you with something?"

The smirk was back on Preston's face, with the same unpleasant curl as the day before, only tighter and with an added malice, and Chase couldn't help but wonder what he'd done to make Preston hate him so much. Then he glanced past the lieutenant and realized Justin was now standing just outside his door, talking on his phone. It seemed the captain had gotten a call and Preston had decided to linger inside long enough to give Justin a moment of privacy. But for the first time, the suspicion brushed the back of Chase's spine that the very thorough and detailed captain who'd questioned him earlier wouldn't do anything without a reason.

His feet planted on the living room floor and his hands clasped behind his back, Chase faced Preston. "Again, can I help you with something? Shouldn't you be taking your son to school?"

"He's with his mother this week." Preston's eyes darted up and down as if he disliked the reminder of his failed marriage.

"Do we have a problem?" Chase asked.

"Apparently, we do." Preston's arms crossed, and for the first time Chase noticed the phone clutched tightly in his hand. "I asked you to stay away from Maisy Lockwood."

Not asked. Told. And it's not like Preston had any right to make that demand of him, let alone issue that order.

"Yes." Chase spoke through gritted teeth. "And I explained very thoroughly already this morning she happened to be at a barbecue I was invited to attend last night."

Preston snorted. "Then do you care to clarify what you were doing holding her hand?"

Chase blinked as the words hit him so hard

he rocked back on his heels. "How on earth could you possibly know that?"

"The whole base knows it!" Preston stuck his phone out, and Chase looked down in shock and horror as the base's anonymous blogger's page filled the screen.

Front and center on the page was a picture of him and Maisy sitting alone on the log. His back was to the camera, but Maisy's face was crystal clear, as were their hands clasped together like two shipwrecked survivors clinging to the wreckage.

A headline ran across the screen: Red Rose Killer Accomplice Finally Found? Is Clint Lockwood's Daughter in a Secret Romantic Relationship with the Man who helped Murder her Father?

All this time the base had been looking for a scapegoat to pin their fears and anger on. Looked like the anonymous blogger had just given them one.

"Maisy! Wait! Stop!" Zoe shouted, running down the sidewalk toward her as Maisy climbed out of her hatchback. The car was bright blue with Sunny Seeds Preschool and happy fruit decals on the side, and today was the first day in memory when the school's small parking lot was so full she wasn't able to pull into her usual spot, forcing her to go around the block and park on the street. Zoe raised both hands in a stopping motion. "Stay there. Don't go anywhere."

"I'm late," Maisy said. She slammed the door and pushed the button on her key fob to hear it lock. She couldn't believe how late. The conversation with Oliver had lasted longer than she'd expected and then it had felt like she'd caught every single red light on the way to school. "The school opens in less than ten minutes, I haven't even set up anything for today and for some reason the parking lot is jammed with cars."

The words hit her ears just as she was saying them. Why was the parking lot full? Yes, it was a small lot and the front of the school did tend to get busy when parents were dropping off children. But there weren't that many students, so the lot was never actually full, unless it was parents' night. Only then did she really look up and see for the first time the scene unfolding in front of her beloved school. People crowded the front of the building. Many were parents and caregivers dropping off students for the day. But there were also the parents of former students and people in uniform she didn't recognize. There was Lieutenant Heidi Jenks, a reporter for CAFB

News, and Yvette Crenville, the base nutritionist, who lived nearby and often came by to talk to the students about healthy eating. Her own classroom assistant teacher, Esther, stood by the front door, along with Bella's classroom assistant, Vance. But through the gap in the brightly patterned curtains she could see Imogene Wilson, the preschool director, talking with Esther's grandfather, Lieutenant General Nathan Hall. Why was the base commander visiting Sunny Seeds?

That's when she noticed Felicity standing halfway down the sidewalk with little Freddy in her arms, and realized she must be holding him so that Zoe could talk to her privately.

Her phone buzzed. It was a text from Ava Esposito.

Are you all right? Praying for you! I'm here if you want to grab coffee or need anything. Hugs!

Fear crept up her spine. What had happened? Another kidnapping? Another Boyd Sullivan sighting? Another creepy rose left by the Red Rose Killer with a threat for someone at Sunny Seeds?

Please, Lord, not another death.

Instinctively, Maisy reached for Zoe's arm. "What happened?"

Sadness washed over her friend's features. "I'm guessing you don't read the Canyon Air Force Base anonymous blogger's website?"

"No, of course not!" Maisy's nose wrinkled instinctively. "Why would I read that trash?"

This was all about gossip? What could the blogger have possibly written that would cause this many people to show up at Sunny Seeds? Heidi looked ready to come her way, but Felicity raised a swift hand and Heidi held back.

Zoe held up her phone. "I'm so sorry about this."

"Just let me see it." She took the phone, glanced down at the screen and felt her heart stop like someone had squeezed it.

It was her. A picture of her sitting on the log in Zoe's backyard, holding Chase's hands.

In the photo, she looked so deeply into Chase's eyes. She looked totally crush-struck. Besotted. She looked like a woman in— No, she wouldn't let herself think that word, the *L* word, not about Chase. Not now. Not ever. Standing there, on the sidewalk, she felt like someone had ripped the door off her heart and left it hanging wide-open for all to see. She pressed her hands, still cool from the car's air-conditioning, against her flaming cheeks. Could everyone tell how she felt about Chase? Could he?

"I'm so sorry," Zoe said. "The blogger has targeted me too and I know what it's like to have the truth of your life twisted up with a whole lot of gossip and innuendo and then used against you."

Her friend's voice was soft, and yet a strength, like battle-tested steel, ran through it, and Maisy suddenly realized why Zoe had been the one of her friends delegated to give her the bad news.

Maisy blinked hard and forced herself to focus on the words written on the screen. The headline was everything she feared it would be, implying in huge bold letters that Chase was Boyd Sullivan's accomplice, and that she was disgracing her father's memory by having an inappropriate and ill-advised romance with the man accused of helping to kill him.

She gritted her teeth and continued reading down the page. The first few paragraphs outlined the case against Chase, including the fact that his name had appeared on a prison visitor log, that Security Forces had raided his home after someone had called in an anonymous report of seeing Boyd Sullivan there and that her father's gold cross had been found after the house was searched. Maisy shook her head. How did the blogger know all that?

Then the blogger had written about the incident of Allie's attempted kidnapping at the school the day before. However, the post twisted the facts around to make it sound like Maisy's class was so badly run that either Allie was a little brat who'd wandered away all on her own, or that Maisy had helped Chase stage the kidnapping in an attempt to paint himself as an innocent victim.

At best, it made Maisy look like a fool who'd been duped by a potential killer. At worse, she was another one of Boyd's accomplices.

The blog trailed on, but she couldn't read another word. Angry tears filled her eyes, briefly blocking out the sea of people surrounding the front of her school.

"It's not fair," Maisy said. "Whoever wrote this is just twisting details, making wild guesses and asking questions, leaving the reader to fill in the answers."

"It's what trolls like that do," Zoe said. "I'm so sorry."

"How did they even know this stuff?" she asked, pushing the phone back into her friend's hand. "Surely, some of these details should be confidential!"

Zoe shook her head, sadness mingled with bewilderment in her eyes.

"I don't know," Zoe admitted. "If you read down to the end of the page, the blogger claims to have a source who anonymously sent the pictures of you and Chase."

She wasn't sure who the anonymous source could possibly be. But whether or not that was true, now the whole world had someone to accuse of being Boyd Sullivan's accomplice. Was the anonymous source the same person who'd cut the screen of Allie's bedroom window and tried to kidnap her?

"So that's why Heidi Jenks is at the school," she said. She'd talked to the reporter briefly after her father had died. Heidi had written a very kind obituary. Maisy knew other people found the tenacious reporter a bit much and some even wondered if Heidi herself was the anonymous blogger. But Maisy had always viewed her as polite, considerate and respectful.

"Heidi and Felicity are neighbors," Zoe said, her lip curled only very slightly to indicate that she and Felicity might not have agreed on the reporter. "Felicity thinks it might be good if you talked to a sympathetic source."

"About what?" Maisy asked. "The fact that someone printed this trash about me? How could this possibly be news?"

"There's an open letter going around among the parents," Zoe said. "It's addressed to Imogene Wilson and the base commander. The parents of almost all the students have signed it."

Fear brushed Maisy's spine. "What kind of letter?"

"I didn't sign it," Zoe said quickly. "You have to know I love you, Freddy loves you and your friends have your back. In fact, some of us are here today as a show of support."

A Security Forces car pulled up behind her with a screech of tires and it took her a second to register Preston's uniformed presence behind the wheel.

"They're demanding armed uniformed Security Forces protection at the front doors," Zoe continued. Maisy nodded. Okay, that wasn't the first time she'd heard that and while she didn't like the idea, she wouldn't be surprised if Imogene caved and agreed to it.

"Okay, and?"

"They want all field trips cancelled, the

back playground and yard closed off and children kept inside all day."

What? Something bristled at the center of her core. Keep the children locked inside all day? Why punish them like that? The thought of their sad little faces pressed up against the window looking out at the glorious Texas sunshine was cruel.

Preston was out of his car and striding toward her now, with a look of determination and purpose she didn't much like. He looked like a rhino preparing to break down a wall.

"Is that it?" Maisy asked.

"They want Allie McLear expelled and Chase forbidden from coming anywhere near the school."

"That's ridiculous!"

"Not if they think Chase is Boyd Sullivan's accomplice and that he set up a fake kidnap attempt yesterday," Zoe said. "They say it's not fair for the school's resources to be diverted to make sure one little girl isn't being used as a pawn, when there are other students to worry about."

Zoe's shoulders rose and fell, and Maisy was reminded that some people had argued she shouldn't have allowed little Freddy in her school either because he was Boyd's nephew. What was wrong with these people? How had fear and paranoia managed to infect the base so deeply? It was like a disease, destroying good will, killing faith and rotting out everything she valued about being part of a base community.

Lord, please, release us from this fear and stop this nightmare before it tears us apart. Help me continue to be a beacon and source of hope, light and comfort to these tiny children, who I know You care for too. Help me continue to do my part to chip away at the darkness.

Zoe took a deep breath. "Sorry, honey, but they're also demanding that you be fired from Sunny Seeds."

NINE

Fired? The word clattered inside Maisy's chest so painfully that for a moment all she could do was stand there, looking in her friend's sad eyes and feeling herself gasp for breath like a fish suddenly yanked from the deep, cool comforts of her pond. Imogene would never fire her. Would she? She was excellent at her job and hadn't taken so much as a day off in years, even after her father had been killed. Surely, the worst-case scenario was that her boss would put her on leave, while they started a long procedure to investigate the complaints against her. Yet, the fact that anyone wanted her to be fired hurt so deeply that it was almost impossible for her to take any comfort in that. This school was her life. Her students were her entire world. Why would anyone try to take that away from her? How could anybody think that her students would be better off without her?

"They can't do this," she said. Her feet feebly and haltingly steered her up toward the front steps and toward the gathering of friends, parents, concerned Canyon residents and those onlookers making somebody else's problem their own. "They can't say I don't care about my students because some scandalous blog decided to write rumors and lies about me, or published a picture of me being seen to…"

Words failed her. Being seen to do what? Hold hands with a criminal suspect. Gaze up into his eyes. Look up at him like he was everything she'd ever wanted and nothing she thought she'd ever be able to have.

"Maisy, we need to talk." Preston barreled to her side. His hand brushed the back of her shoulder and his stiff form fell into step alongside her, as if he'd taken it upon himself to be her personal escort. "Somewhere private."

Nothing in his tone or body language implied it was official. Whatever Preston Flannigan wanted to talk about was way down her list of priorities, and going somewhere private with him was not about to happen.

She shrugged his hand away and kept walking straight ahead without looking at him. "I'm sorry, it'll have to wait. I don't have time right now."

"But you don't know what it's about." He reached for her arm, not exactly touching her, but somehow still uncomfortably close.

"If it's about the Red Rose Killer investigation, please get Captain Blackwood to call me," she said. "I already had a long conversation this morning with FBI Special Agent Oliver Davison."

"It's not police business—"

"Then, please, it has to wait." She raised her head high and walked through the crowd, feeling Zoe close on the other side and seeing Felicity and Heidi ahead. She could hear Preston still talking behind her. Not in coherent sentences though, but blustering and sputtering out syllables like "but," "you" and "I." She didn't turn.

Eyes averted their gaze as she passed. So this was what it was like to have the Canyon Air Force Base's finger of suspicion pointed at you. Suddenly her heart ached for what Zoe had been going through ever since her half brother Boyd had broken out of prison.

And Chase…

She stopped in front of Felicity and Heidi. Zoe reached for Freddy, and Felicity slid the little boy into his mother's arms.

Maisy nodded to Heidi and was relieved to find she still had enough composure to give the journalist a polite smile. "Hi, Heidi. I don't have a statement to make about anything at this time. Okay?"

Despite her reputation for being a ruthless and relentless reporter, Heidi gave her a sympathetic look from behind her large dark-framed glasses. She nodded. "Absolutely."

"Thank you. Are you planning on running a story about me?"

"Not specifically." Heidi's eyes met hers straight on and Maisy found herself thankful for her directness and honesty. "I'm researching a story about Airman Chase McLear. The fact that his daughter was kidnapped from this school will be part of it. But the story has not taken shape yet, so I'll call you for comment before I go to press. In the meantime, feel free to call me anytime if you want to talk, either on or off the record."

She slipped her hand into her pocket and pulled out a business card, and even though Maisy was pretty sure she already had the reporter's number in her phone, she took it and slid it into her pocket. "Thank you."

Heidi disappeared back into the crowd. As Maisy watched her walk away, she noticed Preston talking to Yvette. Whatever he was saying had the very pretty base nutritionist giggling. Looked like the lieutenant had found someone more receptive to his charm.

"Do you want us go into the school with you?" Felicity asked. "I can stick around for a while."

Maisy rolled her shoulders back. Her father's words echoed through her mind. *Strong people fought their own battles*. "No, I'm good."

They paused a moment, then nodded. Zoe shifted Freddy around in her arms.

"Okay, I'm taking Freddy to class," Zoe said. "If you need us, don't hesitate to call."

"Thank you," Maisy said, resisting for the moment the urge to just throw her arms around both friends and hug them. Instead, she stepped back and looked around the chaos on the lawn. Brouhaha or no brouhaha, she was still these children's teacher.

"Esther," she called, raising her tone with her "Miss Maisy voice," as her students called it. "We need to get people sorted through and dropping their kids off. A lot of these people need to get to work. Can you please herd all those dropping their kids into a straight line by the front door? After that, start processing them through into the classroom. As always, parents are welcome to stay with their children if they wish."

Esther nodded and Maisy couldn't help but notice how her usually confident assistant's fingers shook and her dark eyes darted from Maisy's face to the ground and back. Then the younger woman hurried to her side.

"Imogene wants to see you in her office right away," Esther said, confirming what Maisy already suspected. Then her voice dropped. "I didn't tell my grandfather anything bad about what happened yesterday. I promise I didn't, Maisy. But I live with him, while I'm saving up for a house, and he said he was getting flooded with calls and emails this morning from people on base, and around the country, demanding to know why he was letting a 'known threat' near children at the preschool. Even some major civilian news outlets called him, asking for comments about Chase McLear and saying they were sending reporters. He'll be talking to the press later and wanted to talk to you first. Some people are even saying you've been helping Chase by covering up for the fact that he's working with Boyd Sullivan. He can't ignore that."

The national press was showing up at the base to ask if one of Canyon's preschool teachers was, at best, accidentally aiding the

Red Rose Killer's accomplice or, at worse, if she herself was a coconspirator to his crimes? No, she guessed the base commander couldn't just let that go.

"I'm going in the side door," Maisy said. "That will keep the front entrance clear for you to lead the kids into the classroom."

As well, it would give her a few moments alone, in peace and quiet, to pray and ask the Lord for help before stepping inside. Esther nodded. Maisy slipped past the crowd and around the side of the building. She turned the corner, walked a few steps, then stopped and pressed one hand against the wall.

What do I do, Lord? Yes, I know I can dig my heels in. But is that what's best for my students? How do I protect them?

A large hand landed on her shoulder, cutting her prayer short. She spun back, her pulse racing and her arm raised in self-defense as she came within a half-inch of accidentally elbowing Preston across the face. She jumped back. He'd followed her.

"Maisy!" He leaned in. His voice was hushed and urgent. "Before you talk to the base commander we need to talk."

She pressed her lips together as the line she often said to the children crossed her mind—

wanting something wasn't the same as needing it.

"So you've told me." She crossed her arms. "About something personal, that's not official police business. And I've told you it has to wait. So, if you're here as a parent, then either you can accompany your son into the classroom or you can wait for me out front."

"I'm here as a friend," he said quickly. "I'm here because I care about you."

She shook her head. But they weren't friends and Preston couldn't just single-handedly decide they had a personal relationship. He might be drawn to her, in a slightly overbearing way that, truthfully, had always made her feel mildly uncomfortable. In fact, sometimes the teacher's gifts his son gave her at holidays were more generous and personal than she was comfortable with. Had she done something to let him think she was open to a deeper relationship with him? Did she need to be bolder at putting him in his place?

But he was a member of the Security Forces, the father of one of her students and someone investigating her father's murder.

"Now is not a good time. I will talk to you later, Preston."

She reached for the side door. He stepped

in front of her. "Tell me you're not involved with Chase McLear!"

The words flew out of his mouth, more like an order than a question.

"Excuse me?" Who did this man think he was? She drew herself up to her full height, even as she knew how slight it was. "My personal life is none of your business!"

"Well, maybe it should be." He stepped closer. "There's something bad going down on base and you need someone to protect you." His hand touched her shoulder. "And it should be me."

There were too many cars and people around the front of the school, Chase thought as he pulled his truck past Sunny Seeds. His eyes scanned the road. In the back seat, Allie was chirping away to Queenie in a silly little made-up language of hers that only the dog seemed to understand. If only he understood her as well as his own canine partner did. His heart ached and he let it turn into a prayer for wisdom.

Help me. Please. I feel like I'm all alone, not knowing what I'm guarding, being attacked on all sides and not knowing what to do. Help me to remember that You are my sword and my shield of protection.

"Daddy! We go pass Sunny Seeds!" Allie's voice piped up from the back seat.

"I know, Sweet Pea," he said. He palmed the steering wheel around the corner. "We're just running a little late and I need to find a place to park."

Truth be told, he'd been hoping to keep Allie home and spare her the chaos.

Coming so close to losing her—and knowing how close he still was to losing Queenie—had made him wake up determined to hold her close to his chest and never let her go. Instead, she'd been so insistent on going to see Maisy, she'd practically dragged him out the door once he'd gotten her fed and coaxed her into wearing summer clothes.

Honestly, he couldn't blame her. Something inside of him understood the desire to be around Maisy. If he'd been a different man, in a different place in time and not facing all that he was going through, when he'd collected a sleeping Allie from her arms in the living room the night before, he'd have asked Maisy out on a first date. And when they'd been sitting all alone in the backyard, with his hands enveloping hers and her eyes looking into his, he might have even asked if he could kiss her.

Instead, the blog post Preston had angrily

waved in his face had been a glaring reminder that all he could bring to Maisy's life was pain and conflict. She deserved better. She deserved better than a man like him, in a mess like his life was in, and better than the further chaos he'd bring to her life.

There were far more people around the front of the preschool than usual and his heart lurched with worry as he pondered the reason.

He eased his vehicle around the corner, looking to park on a side street. Then he heard shouting. He looked out the window and what he saw made his foot hit the break as hard as he dared without jolting Allie and Queenie. Preston, standing with his chest puffed out and hands raised, was yelling at Maisy. Chase couldn't make out his words but it didn't matter—there was no way he was going to just sit there and watch her get berated.

He opened the door and leaned out, one boot hitting the pavement the moment he cut the engine. "Hey! Leave her alone!"

Preston turned sharply. His face went red, like a cartoon steam engine barely managing to contain itself from exploding. Maisy's eyes met Chase's for one long and grateful moment, and his breath caught at the vulnerability in her face. Then she turned and disappeared through Sunny Seeds' side door.

Preston's hands balled into fists. He started across the grass toward where Chase still sat, halfway out of his truck.

Chase glanced back at Queenie. "Stay! Watch Allie!"

He stepped out of the vehicle, leaving the door open, and leaned against the back door, creating a physical barrier between Preston and his precious daughter. He slid his hand behind him through the open window and felt for Allie's tiny shoulder, so she'd know her daddy was there.

"What are you doing here?" Preston demanded, punctuating the question with a swear word that snapped from his lips so suddenly it was like a whip cracking in the air.

"Watch your language in front of my daughter," Chase said, "and lower your voice."

"You should get back in the truck and take her home." Preston scowled. Something about what Chase said must've tweaked something inside Preston's conscience because his voice lowered. "It's not right for you to be here when you're under criminal investigation. There's a letter going around from people demanding that Maisy suspend Allie from school and that you be banned from school property until your name is cleared."

He wondered if it was started by Preston. Something twisted like the tip of a knife in the pit of Chase's stomach. How dare anyone try to punish a little girl for something they imagined her father had done? But then, the lieutenant added something that made the pain cut even deeper. "They're also demanding that Maisy be fired from Sunny Seeds because they suspect she must be helping you, which would mean that either knowingly or unknowingly, she's also helping the Red Rose Killer. Not that I personally think she'd ever intentionally do anything criminal. She's too sweet and innocent to get messed up in crime on purpose. But parents are demanding the preschool director do something and the base commander has been threatened with large-scale protests in front of Canyon."

Chase felt his right hand slide over his heart. No, they couldn't threaten Maisy. Not because of him. Her job was the most important thing in the world to her and she was incredible at it. Surely, her boss knew that. That anyone would harass her, threaten her or try to take anything away from her because of him hurt him deeply. Liz had always accused him of robbing her of the life she'd really wanted and now he was going to do the same to Maisy. He slumped back against the vehicle, as if his legs no longer knew how to hold him. Then he felt Allie's hand reach up, grab his fingers and squeeze him tightly.

"I can't believe you'd do that to Maisy," Chase said. "She doesn't deserve any of this."

Preston's chest rose and his face was a mixture of both pride and absolute certainty. There was nothing worse than someone who thought he was right all the time. Chase wondered what it was like to go through life that confident. He supposed it would make life easier for him, but harder for everyone around him.

"I'm doing this for Maisy," Preston said. "I care about Maisy way more than you could ever understand. She needs me to protect her from herself."

Did she now? Chase nearly snorted. He couldn't believe it. Preston thought he cared about Maisy. He might even think he loved her. Because he was selfish enough to think the fact that he was attracted to her meant something. For a moment, the question of whether Preston's determination to find Chase guilty had something to do with Maisy hovered in Chase's mind. Except Chase and Maisy had never so much as gone out for coffee together, let alone had a personal relationship, and Preston's furious grilling of him had happened before the barbecue.

Besides, how could anyone be foolish enough to think a woman as smart, kind and beautiful as Maisy would ever be with a man like him?

Something soured in Preston's gaze, as if reading Chase's mind.

"Believe it or not," Preston said, "I'm only after the truth."

No, he didn't believe it. "I'm sure you think that's true. But I don't."

He watched as Preston's fists clenched even tighter and wondered if he was going to have to block a physical punch in front of his little girl. But then, Preston turned and stormed off with a determination and anger that left Chase with no doubt he'd be back with an even harder and more impactful blow.

Chase waited until he disappeared around the corner, then he opened the vehicle door and pulled Allie into his arms.

"He was loud, Daddy," she said.

"I know, Sweet Pea." He sighed. "I'm so sorry you had to hear him."

Her little hand brushed his cheek. "You okay, Daddy?"

"No," he said honestly. "His yelling made

me sad. But you and I and Queenie are going to play together in the grass for a bit, while we wait to see if Maisy is okay."

She nodded wisely. "Maisy is im-por-tant, right, Daddy?"

He hugged her tightly. Yes, Maisy was important. She was important to him in ways he didn't know how to put into words. And what kind of person was he to bring such pain and chaos into her life? His first impulse yesterday had been right. He had to pull Allie from Maisy's school. He had to disappear from her life completely until the dust settled and stop making his problems hers. He'd wait until the crowd cleared, then he'd quietly speak to Maisy in person and tell her what he'd decided. He'd do it before she could ask. He owed her that much.

He didn't have that long to wait. He and Allie had barely started their fourth round of I Spy when the side door opened and a small blonde figure slipped through. Instinctively, he stood and his arms reached for her. "Maisy, are you okay?"

"No." Her gaze traveled past him to the horizon. "I'm on vacation. I had some time available to use up and when I realized just how challenging it would be for my students if I dug my heels in, I offered to take it. My boss agrees it's the easiest way to calm the situation down short term. She will get a really good supply teacher to come in to help Esther cover my class, and I'll come back later this evening, once the school is closed, to lay out lesson plans for the next few days."

"I'm so sorry. Is there anything I can do?"

Her eyes turned toward him and he realized she was fighting back tears.

"Yes, Chase, please take me somewhere, anywhere, far away from here."

TEN

The words hung in the air between them, her incredibly honest plea waiting to be answered.

"I'm sorry," she said. "I'm not sure where that came from. But there's still a crowd of people out front, and the base commander warned me more press might be coming..."

Her words faded on her lips as Allie ran across the lawn and threw her arms around Maisy's legs in a tackle hug.

"Don't be sad, Maisy," Allie said. "Daddy says you're im-por-tant."

"You and your daddy are important too," Maisy whispered, as she reached down and ran her hand over Allie's curls. Then she looked up. Chase was looking at her, with that same intensity that she'd seen in his eyes the night before. For a moment, they just stood there, looking at each other, as if neither of them knew what to say.

"There's a wonderful little waterfall, on a very public path, just half an hour off base," Chase said. "I was thinking of taking Allie and Queenie for a hike. Obviously, I'll call Captain Blackwood to tell him before I leave base. But it's got good trails and it's far away from anywhere investigators think Boyd Sullivan might be hiding out. We could pack a picnic. What do you say? Do you want to join us?"

She could feel the smile that spread across her face as something exploded inside her chest like a shower of sparklers on the Fourth of July. "That would be lovely. If you don't mind swinging by my house first, I have a basket we could use."

"Sounds good." Half a grin curled up at the corner of his mouth, with a look that was somewhere in between handsome and cute. Then he glanced down at Allie. "If that's okay with you, Sweet Pea?"

Allie nodded. She slipped her hand into Maisy's, and they walked back to the truck. Maisy helped Allie get settled in as Chase made a quick phone call to Justin.

"All clear," Chase said. "He agrees with my assessment that the trails by the waterfall are far too public for someone like Boyd Sullivan to be camped out near, and they've been well-monitored by police recently. We're good to go."

They took his truck and left her car parked in front of Sunny Seeds, still surrounded by people on the sidewalk, gawking, gossiping and demanding answers that neither of them had.

"I'm guessing you know about the blog?" Maisy asked after a long moment.

"I do." He nodded. "I know about the letter the parents wrote too and the calls to the base commander."

"And you know about Frank Golosky's brother, Drew?" she asked softly.

"I do." He nodded gravely. "I was questioned about it this morning."

She should've known he would be. "Is it possible he's the 'hurt man' Allie has been talking about?"

"I don't see how that could be possible. Allie's been having these nightmares for weeks," Chase said. He eased the truck to a stop at a stop sign and glanced at her. "Are you okay?"

"Not really," she said. "I just want a break from all this—from the fear, the suspicion and the panic. It's like we've been in perpetual crisis mode for months, and I just want it to stop."

"I understand," he said. He reached over and brushed her hand. "So let's give ourselves a break, just for today, and let ourselves have fun."

"I'd like that." She felt a smile cross her lips. Then she glanced up at the rearview mirror at the little girl in the back seat. "And how do you think we should have fun on our picnic, Allie?"

She listened as Allie chatted happily about all the random and interesting thoughts going through her mind. Chase drove them through the checkpoint gates and off the base. She directed them to her little bungalow and felt an odd mixture of nerves and pride as she invited them into her home, with its brightly colored walls and beautifully messy framed artwork by former students. They set up shop in her sunny yellow kitchen, where she turned on the radio to something upbeat, put a brightly handled picnic basket on the kitchen table and filled the counter with breads, cheeses, cold cuts and vegetables. She left Chase and Allie to get started making a picnic and went to get changed.

"Maisy's happy," Allie chirped as Maisy turned the corner into the hall. "I like it when Maisy is happy!"

"Me too," Chase said.

Joy swelled in Maisy's heart like an old friend that she'd thought she'd lost forever. She was truly and deeply happy in a way she never thought she'd feel again.

Lord, how can I be happy when my world is falling apart? How can I feel this happy when all our lives are in crisis and the base is under a constant shroud of fear? How can both joy and sadness—hope and fear—coexist inside my heart?

She emerged a few minutes later, in well-worn jeans, a short-sleeved blue plaid shirt and a pink bandanna holding back her hair. Her eyes ran over the mess that man and child had made of her usually pristine kitchen. Chase's mouth opened and then closed again. His hand ran over his head and his face reddened slightly.

"Are you all right?" she said. "Look, if it's about the mess, don't worry about it. It won't take us long to clean if we work together."

"It's not the kitchen," Chase said. His shoulders straightened. "You just look really good. Better than good. Beautiful."

The feelings that crowded her heart swelled so suddenly she gasped to breathe. Did he have any idea how attractive she found him? How impressive he was in her eyes? Not just the outer shell, with his broad chest and strong arms, his kind mouth and the way his green eyes dazzled like a lake in the sun. But the way he cared for his daughter. The way he held his head high and didn't let himself fall into either anger or self-pity the way so many other men would in his situation. The way he'd come to her rescue when she'd needed a hero, if even just for a day.

"You look im-por-tant," Allie added.

Maisy smiled.

"Thank you," she said, pulling her eyes away from the father and focusing on the daughter. She reached into her pocket and pulled out a second bandanna. "I was wondering if you'd like to wear one of these too. I thought we could match."

"Yes!" Allie wriggled off the chair and ran toward her. Gently, her fingers brushed Allie's curls back behind her ears, her heart suddenly aching for the toddler. They sang silly songs as they cleaned the kitchen and packed the last of the food. It was a half-hour drive to the trails and yet, there was something about being there in Chase's truck with him and Allie that seemed to make the drive fly by.

When they reached the trails and climbed out of the truck, Chase clipped the lead on Queenie's harness, slung the picnic basket over his shoulder and then, to her surprise, reached for Maisy's hand. His fingers brushed hers. Her hand slipped instinctively into his. Then Chase seemingly caught himself and pulled away. "Sorry… I wasn't… I didn't…"

"Don't worry about it," she said. "I'm a preschool teacher. Somebody's always grabbing my hand."

But even as she said the lighthearted words, her heart skipped a beat to realize just how natural the movement had been for her too.

"I like holding hands!" Allie announced, stepping in between them. She grabbed her father with one hand and Maisy with the other, holding them tightly, like the tiny link joining them.

Maisy squeezed her hand gently. "Thank you, Allie. I like holding hands with you too."

They walked through the trees and down the wide path, exploring rocks, stumps and the streams that were all but dried up in Texas's July sun. When that sun had risen high in the sky, they reached the bottom of the waterfall, spread Chase's old military blanket and Maisy's quilt side by side under a canopy of trees and shared a happy, simple meal together.

There was a four-foot tall lean-to made of crisscrossed sticks propped up nearby that looked like it had been made by a previous family with small children. After Chase had checked it thoroughly, making sure it was well-constructed and clean of debris, he agreed to Allie's pleas to let her play house inside it. Queenie lay across the entrance, her eyes closed and ears twitching at every happy noise the child made. Maisy reached into the picnic basket and pulled out a spare set of plastic cutlery and dishes. Then she pretended to tap on the side of Allie's hut. "Knock, knock."

Allie's head popped out. "Can I help you?"

Maisy pressed her lips together to keep from laughing. "I was wondering if you'd like these."

Allie's eyes grew wide. Her arms stretched out to take all of the dishes at once. Maisy carefully helped arrange everything in her tiny hands. Allie beamed and disappeared back into her hut.

"What do you say?" Chase called.

"Thank you, Maisy!"

Maisy laughed. So did Chase. He sat down on the blanket and leaned back against a log.

"She's amazing," Maisy said. She carefully put the lids back on the plastic containers and placed them back in her basket. "I can't imagine anyone not wanting to—" Her hands rose to her lips, feeling herself catch the words before they flew out of her mouth.

I can't imagine anyone not wanting to be her mother.

"What were you going to say?" Chase asked.

"Never mind." She knelt on the blanket and closed the picnic basket. "I was going to say something that's really none of my business."

"Maybe I want you in my business." He leaned forward and grabbed her hands.

She slid her fingers from his grasp. "I will listen to anything you want to tell me, Chase. But I'm not going to pry."

"Fair enough." He sat back. "I was hoping you were going to ask me about Allie's mother. Because I've been wanting to talk to you about her, but I'm not exactly good at opening up."

She sat beside him and stretched her short legs out next to his long ones. "What happened?"

"I heard somewhere once that we only accept as much love from other people as we think we deserve," he said. "I don't know if that's true. But I think I always knew on some level that there was something wrong with my relationship with Liz. It was as if she didn't like the person I was, that if she nitpicked me enough she could turn me into the man she wanted me to be. But her criticisms made me shut down even more. Our marital problems drove me back to church, to my faith in God and to dedicating myself to being the kind of man God wanted me to be. But Liz went the other direction. We tried counseling and she very reluctantly agreed to try for a child, I think, because she was surprised to realize how strong my feelings were about being a father. She said it was the first thing she really believed I cared about."

He glanced over to where Allie was happily playing in her makeshift house.

"She got pregnant when I was home on leave," he said, "then while I was stationed back in Afghanistan, she fell in love with somebody else. The marriage was over before Allie was born and Liz hasn't ever tried to see her since then. Her new husband didn't want to help raise another man's child, so I got full custody. I can't regret my relationship with Liz, because if it weren't for her, I wouldn't have Allie. But I worry I'm not a good enough dad to her. Westley told me last night that if the mess my life is in doesn't get cleared up soon, I might lose Queenie, and as much as I love my career, the worst part about it will be telling Allie. She'll be devastated."

Maisy grabbed his hand and squeezed it so tightly he blinked.

"You're an amazing dad, Chase," she said. "You have the biggest heart when it comes to her and it shines through your eyes. I don't think love like that can be faked. I really don't."

She held his hand for one long heartbeat. Then she let go and leaned back again, her shoulder just barely brushing his.

"I don't know what your father was like growing up," Chase said. "But he reminded me a lot of my grandfather. Grandpa was former military intelligence and moved in with us when my father was stationed overseas. He was a firm believer in controlling your emotions and not letting anything get to you, ever. I broke my leg when I was four and he gave me this big stack of comics in the hospital. He told me that I was a hero like them and that heroes never cried."

"Jesus cried at Lazarus's tomb," Maisy said. "I know my father cried when my mother died. He hid it from me, but I could tell. He'd go for long runs through the ravine alone and when he came back, his eyes would be red."

"Maisy, you've got to believe me when I say I have no idea how your father's cross turned up at my house," Chase said. "I would never do anything to hurt your father. I would never knowingly hurt anyone. I wouldn't. I couldn't."

Tears pricked at the edges of her eyelids. Her heart believed him, just like her heart was convinced that he'd never do anything that would risk hurting his child. But her brain just had too many unanswered questions.

If Chase was innocent, then why hadn't Justin cleared his name? Was it possible that Boyd Sullivan was the "bad man" who haunted Allie's nightmares? If so, who was the "hurt man" and how had Allie become so frightened?

"I've never told anybody this," he added. "But when I was in junior high, I was on the school wrestling team and I accidentally broke a smaller guy's fingers. Everyone knew it was an accident. But it was a wake-up call to me that I always had to be careful, because someone my size could hurt someone smaller without meaning to. I had a hard time forgiving myself and I never let myself forget that I had a responsibility to use my strength to help, not hurt."

She nestled closer to him, until her shoulder, her arm and the back of her hand were all brushing against him. Then their fingers gently, slowly touched.

"Maisy," Chase said softly. "I promise you, I will do everything in my power to protect you and keep you from ever being hurt, by me or anyone else, ever again."

Tears welled suddenly at the edges of her eyes, spilling down her cheeks. She wasn't even sure why she was crying. All she knew was that all her life she'd waited to hear a man say something like that to her, and he was the first.

"My father was a good man," Maisy said, "and I know he must've loved me. But he was walled off too, especially after my mother died. I have no memories of him hugging me or telling me he was proud of me. I never thought he liked who I was."

Suddenly, the need for a hug was stronger than her need to hold back. Her arms slid around his neck. His arms wrapped around her back. He held her, tightly, hugging her to his chest.

"Hey, it's okay," he whispered. His cheek brushed against the top of her head. "Trust me, Maisy. Your father loved you."

"So everybody keeps telling me," she said. She let her head fall against his shoulder. The scent of him filled her senses. “How can you possibly know?”

“Because I still remember the day I first laid eyes on you,” he said. He pulled back, just enough that she could look in his eyes. “I asked Frank Golosky who the beautiful blond dynamite girl was reading by the mess hall. He laughed and said you were Clint Lockwood’s daughter and that guys like me shouldn’t stare too long if we valued our hide, because your father would kill anyone who so much as looked at you funny. He said your father would’ve protected you over his own career if it came to that. So I needed to get in my head fast that the most gorgeous person I’d ever laid eyes on was off-limits to normal grunts like me.”

“Really?” Her eyes grew wide. “So that’s why no nice guys ever asked me out? Because they were afraid of my father?”

“Probably some of them,” he admitted. His hands tightened around her. “But the smart ones had to know they weren’t good enough for you. You deserve the best, Maisy. You really do. You can’t imagine how many times I’ve looked at you and wished I could be the kind of man you deserve.”

She leaned toward him. The gap between them closed. Then their lips touched, softly and gently, and she wasn't sure if he kissed her or if she kissed him. It was like they'd just been swept toward each other by the same invisible current. But here she was, feeling Chase's arms around her and his lips on hers.

His phone rang, loud and shrill in his pocket, with an urgency that demanded to be heard. They sprang apart. "Hello. McLear here."

He stood. So did she. Her eyes darted to the wooden shelter. Allie was still playing happily inside, babbling to herself.

Maisy breathed a sigh of relief. What had she been thinking? What if Allie had seen?

"Got it," Chase said. "It'll take me about an hour, but I'll be there." He hung up and turned to Maisy. "That was Master Sergeant James. He wants me to come to the K-9 training center immediately."

The sun had started its descent in the afternoon sky as Chase pulled the truck back onto the base. Hiking back down had taken longer than he'd expected, thanks to Allie's unwillingness to leave her new "tree home." Then she'd fallen asleep in the back seat of the truck, leaving an odd, uncomfortable silence filling the front seat between him and Maisy, as if the memory of the kiss they'd shared had spread a field of invisible landmines between them.

Had that really happened? Had he really held Maisy Lockwood in his arms and kissed her? It felt like a dream, one that he was afraid to wake up from. He wondered if he should apologize, and yet she'd kissed him back. She'd clung to him just as tightly as he'd held her.

"I'll drop you off at Sunny Seeds, so you can pick up your car," he said. "Then I'll head to the training center."

"I'll watch Allie," Maisy said. "I'll take her into Sunny Seeds with me. I told Imogene I'd drop back later in the day to pick up a few personal things and make sure I left Esther and the supply teacher some notes about the class."

It was a plan that made sense and one for which he was grateful.

"Okay," he said. He had no idea what Westley wanted, but he couldn't shake the threat hanging over his head of losing Queenie. It was like the phone call had sucked all the hope from his heart and the oxygen from his lungs, leaving him with nothing but the nagging questions he didn't begin to have answers to.

How was he ever going to find Ajay Joseph, barring flying to Afghanistan personally and searching the mountains for his village? If Ajay had been so concerned about possible theft in his crew, why had he just dropped the issue? Yes, he'd emailed to say he was mistaken and no crime had been committed. Plus, there'd been a family emergency. But he'd seemed so distraught about it when they'd talked. Captain Dennis's email said that Ajay had left his job as a civilian liaison and Ajay hadn't even called Chase to explain the mix-up and follow up about the files he'd emailed. None of it squared with how dedicated he knew Ajay was to his men. The thought of putting in another call to Captain Reardon or even popping by her office niggled at the back of his mind. She and Captain Dennis had always seemed close. Perhaps she could urge him to dig deeper? Yet, her warning that anyone who came too near Chase was at risk of having his or her reputation tarred gave him pause. What Maisy was going through was all too much evidence that she'd been right.

Then there was the matter of Preston's personal vendetta against him, who the figure in the hood was who'd tried to kidnap Allie and why a respected captain like Justin Blackwood hadn't yet figured out who the person was who'd framed him. Thoughts leaped in his brain like sizzling bacon fat and he couldn't get anywhere close to finding answers without someone he cared about getting burned.

The lights were off and the parking lot was empty when he pulled up in front of Sunny Seeds. The crowd had moved on, for now.

"There's a bed in a side room just off the main office," Maisy said. "She can nap there."

He cradled his sleeping daughter to his chest, carried Allie up to the preschool and waited while Maisy unlocked the doors. She led them through the darkened and silent preschool, into the small room he guessed was an infirmary. She gestured to a child-sized bed. "You can lay her down there."

He eased his daughter from his arms, brushed a kiss on the top of her head and turned to Maisy.

"Thank you," he whispered. "I don't know what Westley wants, but I'm hoping I won't be long."

"Bad man! Hurt man! No!" Allie's panicked wail shook the silence, tearing his heart in half.

He turned back. But Maisy was one step ahead of him.

"It's okay, Allie, you're safe." Maisy dropped

down to the bedside. She glanced up at Chase and waved a hand to indicate he could go. “It’s okay. She’s still asleep. It’s just a nightmare. I’ve got this.”

Didn’t she hear his daughter’s terrified wail? Didn’t she see the hidden pain shaking her little body? Maisy began to sing tenderly to his daughter, a simple little song about sowing the seeds of faith. Her fingers ran gently down Allie’s arms. As he watched, his little girl’s cries faded and she nestled into Maisy’s arms.

“It’s okay, Chase,” Maisy said again, her voice barely rising about a whisper. “You can go. I’ll take care of her.”

A lump formed in his throat as he watched Maisy cradle his daughter. It was like, for the first time, he was seeing something he’d always wanted but never thought he’d find. The longing of hundreds of lonely days and empty nights crashed over him.

He walked slowly out of the preschool, with Queenie at his heels, and drove home to get changed into his uniform. Two television news vans were parked in front of his house. He pulled into the driveway past a handful of people, who by the looks of things were both reporters and random gawkers waiting around, hoping for a show. He wondered if they'd left Sunny Seeds when they discovered Maisy had left on vacation or if they'd stuck around all day, until school ended and the last of the staff had left for the day.

He clipped Queenie's lead on her harness, got out of the truck and shut the door so hard the vehicle shook. The anonymous blogger had spilled the can of worms that up to that point hadn't spread too far beyond base gossip. After almost four months of deaths and fear, the blogger had finally given the world what it wanted—a prime suspect.

He walked through the gauntlet of people shouting questions and pointing cameras at his face, went into his home, got changed into his uniform and then repeated the same walk back to his truck, keeping his head high and his composure in place. Then he drove through the base to the K-9 training center. One of the news vans followed immediately. He wondered if the other one eventually would too or if they'd continue to stake out his house. A deep, sad sigh moved through his body.

He hated this whole mess and could only pray he'd eventually find a way out.

A dozen memories clashed inside him as he eased his truck into the familiar lot in front of the K-9 training center. He remembered what it had felt like the first time he'd driven there, for his initial interview with Westley to see about joining the team, and the hope that had filled his heart. He remembered the excitement and challenge of coming day after day for training, and those seemingly endless days after his training had been completed when he'd waited to find out if he'd been assigned a dog. Then the elating moment he'd gotten the call from Westley, telling him there was a little beagle named Queenie he wanted Chase to meet. He remembered the day he and Queenie had shown up to train, only to be sent back home again on suspension.

When the engine stopped, he rested his hands on the steering wheel and prayed, asking God for help as worries welled up inside him. Then he led Queenie across the parking lot before the reporters had made it out of their van. Queenie's ears perked. Her footsteps quickened until he could tell she was fighting the urge to tug him toward the building. She loved her K-9 training so much; it would be unfair of him to stand in her way if she was able to get another trainer.

He texted Westley. The former head trainer came and met him by the door, with Dakota by his side. The two men exchanged greetings and salutes.

"Thank you for coming," Westley said. Chase expected him to lead him into either the kennels or the offices. Instead, Westley turned and led him toward the veterinary building next door. "Who's watching your daughter?"

"Maisy," Chase said. "She and I went hiking with Allie today. I'm sorry for not being here sooner. It took me a lot longer to get back than I expected."

Westley cut him a sideways glance and his eyebrows rose. Then they walked for another long minute, as if the K-9 trainer was weighing his words.

"Two more of the lost dogs, which Boyd Sullivan let out of the kennels in April, were found late last night," he said, after a long moment. "We've suspected that the dogs that are still missing are either injured or have PTSD, because otherwise they would've returned to the base by now."

He stopped in front of a glass window and pointed. Chase looked through. There, huddled together on a soft bed of blankets were two German shepherds. The larger of the two had been shaved on one side and dark stitches showed stark against the skin. The smaller dog had a cast on her leg and was shaking so hard Chase felt sympathy ricochet through his bones.

"Julius is the big one with the black fur and Penelope is the one who's a mixture of brown and black," Westley said, and Chase was surprised that he could keep his voice so level. "They're both Afghanistan service dogs. Apparently, they stuck together. Penelope was a bomb-sniffing dog, who survived a shell attack on the field and had pretty bad PTSD as a result. Our head vet, Captain Kyle Roark, thinks she broke her leg during their escape from the kennels in April. Our best guess is that Julius looked out for her, protected her and brought her food. Not sure where he got the injuries, but they were pretty deep and seem to be from some kind of wild animal attack. Searchers found him first and he was unwilling to leave her. It was touch and go for a while if Penelope would have to lose her leg, but it looks like she came through surgery like a champ."

Chase felt his hand ball into a fist.

These dogs were United States Air Force service members. They were partners. They saved the lives of men and women in uniform.

How could anyone believe he'd have anything to do with this?

He could feel the emotional weight of it

all bearing down on him. Allie was having nightmares. Maisy's life had been thrown into chaos. Queenie was missing out on her training. Reporters had shown up at his home. And now, seeing these two beautiful and majestic dogs recovering from such injuries was one thing more that he could not bear.

He closed his eyes tightly and prayed, as he fought to maintain composure.

How much longer, Lord? How long do I have to withstand this? When will this trial be over? When will my salvation come?

Westley's voice dug at him like a knife. "Did you help Boyd Sullivan do this?"

"Of course not!" Chase slapped the wall, feeling the sting of his bare hand on the plaster. Despite what his grandfather might have drilled into him as a little boy, sometimes heroes didn't maintain their composure, as Maisy had reminded him by pointing out that Jesus cried. Well, Jesus had gotten emotional and shouted too sometimes.

"I don't know if you brought me here to accuse me, trick me or try to trap me!" Chase turned and faced Westley full-on. "But I give you my word, as a man, an airman and a father, that I had absolutely nothing to do with what happened to those beautiful animals. I love and respect my country, my uniform, the men, women and canines I serve alongside, and my own daughter too much to ever do anything to help Boyd Sullivan."

"What if he threatened you?" Westley crossed his arms. "Or blackmailed you?"

Chase's chin rose. "Then I'd sooner face it head-on than do anything that made me ashamed to look my daughter in the eye."

Silence spread between the two men, long and deep, like that of two airmen, weapons at the ready in no man's land, trying to determine who was friend and who was foe.

Then Westley's shoulders relaxed.

"I'm recommending a reassessment of Queenie at the end of next week," he said. "Then we can determine if Queenie needs to restart any of her training, and if she should be reassigned. I'm hoping the matters you're dealing with will be resolved by then. It appears you and she have a solid connection and it would be good if you could stay partners."

Did this mean Westley believed he was innocent? Or that he was at least willing to give him the benefit of the doubt? Either way, it was a bigger vote of confidence than he'd felt in a while.

"Thank you," he said. "Hopefully this will all be over soon."

"Hopefully," Westley agreed. They walked

back through the building, with his Queenie trotting on one side and Westley's Dakota on the other.

"One more thing," Westley said as they reached the door. "Maisy is like family to Felicity and me. There are a lot of us who would hate to see anyone hurt her."

"Yes, sir." Chase nodded. "Believe me, I would hate to see her hurt as well."

"It's good we understand each other."

Chase waited in the entranceway to the building for a long moment after Westley had walked away and braced himself, hoping he wouldn't have to face a fresh throng of reporters outside. Then he stepped outside, glanced at his truck and frowned. A second news van had joined the first one. Four reporters, two with cameras, clustered around his truck. Thankfully, they didn't seem to have noticed him yet and he didn't much feel like walking past them. Hopefully, the fact that they'd followed him here meant they were no longer staking out his house. He was only a twenty-minute walk from Sunny Seeds. If he left his truck at the training center, walked to pick up Allie and walked her home, he might be able to slip in his back door before the phalanx of reporters caught up with him again. Of course, then he'd have the problem of how to come back and pick his truck up later. But he could only handle one thing at a time and right now, something inside him was itching to just walk and clear his head.

He turned sharply and led Queenie between the K-9 training center and veterinary building, then started strolling through the quiet base backstreets. To his left lay the church where he'd sat in the back during Maisy's father's funeral in April, his heart twisting in knots as he'd seen the tears in Maisy's eyes, and the training facilities where he'd sweated through basic training many years earlier, all while those same dazzling blue eyes did a number on his heart. Just like the memory of kissing Maisy by the waterfall was making that same sorry heart beat something fierce inside his chest now.

He cut right and walked along the perimeter fence that separated the base from the woods. He'd never imagined it was even possible to miss someone who he'd spent the day with and seen just an hour ago. And yet, he missed Maisy, as if a part of his own heart was hers. Would reporters be camped outside her home too? How would she feel when she woke up in the morning and had no job to go to, and gossip reporters questioning if she'd helped her own father's killer?

Ahead loomed the large warehouse complex that housed equipment, weapons, vehicles and supplies to be shipped by truck, plane and boat to Afghanistan. He'd once had an office in the very middle of that complex before he'd started his K-9 training, when he was still responsible for ensuring the security of shipments. His former boss, Captain Jennifer Reardon, worked in there now. Would she still be in her office? Had she had any progress in accessing Ajay Joseph's files? It was a shot in the dark. But sometimes that was the only type of shot left to take.

He turned and led Queenie toward the building. They entered the comforting coolness of the warehouse. A block of offices sat deep inside the expansive building with large windows looking out into the warehouse, as if someone had plucked a single floor off a regular office building and dropped it in the middle of a sea of forklifts, equipment and loading bays. The building was mostly empty, but even as he passed, the few airmen and support staff that were still on the floor seemed to avert their gaze. What would he have seen if he'd looked in their faces? Suspicion? Doubt? Hostility? Or just confusion? Was this how it would always be? Walking through his former life like a ghost of the man he used to be?

He reached the offices. Captain Reardon's light was still on. Through the half-pulled blinds of her huge office window, he could see two figures. Looked like she was in a meeting.

His footsteps paused a few paces from her office door. He'd wait.

A yip dragged his attention back down to his feet. Queenie tugged hard on her leash and whimpered with that little whine of impatience that told him she smelled something important and wanted to go search for it. She'd been like that when he'd first started training her. He'd had to drill into her that she only searched on command and not whenever she smelled something she thought she was supposed to find. Beagles had one of the best noses for tracking and he knew they could tracks things over long distances. But he couldn't imagine how many laptops, computers, cell phones and electronic storage devices were in these offices, not to mention the warehouse. Did this mean she was forgetting her training already? He could only hope all the progress she'd made wouldn't be lost because of him.

"Leave it," he said. "When we get home, we can train."

She tugged harder, pulling him toward Captain Reardon's office door. She looked up at him, eager and impatient. Then she howled, with a yelp that was a mixture of urgency and excitement.

The office blind moved back. The calm, calculating gaze of Captain Justin Blackwood met his through Captain Reardon's office window. So, at least one of the men investigating him was in his former boss's office. Queenie's howls grew louder and sharper, echoing through the warehouse. More faces appeared at other office windows now, making him feel like even more of a spectacle. Justin's eyebrows rose, just as heat rose to the back of Chase's neck. His cell phone began to ring, its tinny sound combining with the cacophony of his frantic dog.

He glanced at the screen. It was Maisy.

"Come on." He tugged Queenie's lead. "We'll go wait for Captain Reardon outside."

The phone stopped ringing. He suspected the call had dropped. Cell phone reception had always been lousy in the warehouse, not that Maisy would be able to hear him anyway, with Queenie kicking up a fuss. Queenie was still yipping as he firmly led her back through the warehouse toward the exit.

What had he been thinking just showing up at her office like that? He'd probably shot whatever remaining credibility he had with Captain Blackwood by showing what little control he had over his canine. He slipped back outside into the evening light and leaned against the wall. Queenie had gone quiet. He looked down. Her ears drooped.

"What was that all about?" he asked. "What did you smell that was so important?"

His phone started ringing again. He answered. "Hello?"

"Hey, Chase." Maisy's voice was faint and yet something about it sent warmth spreading through his core. "Allie's awake and I'm done here. I was wondering when you were going to be back and if you wanted me to figure out something for dinner. I could take Allie back to my place and cook us something."

Did she have any idea how much he'd have enjoyed that? He was less than a ten-minute walk from Sunny Seeds now. He could probably run it in under five.

"Thanks for the offer, but I'll be there soon to take her home," he said. "There were reporters in front of my house and the K-9 training center. So you might want to keep the curtains shut and plan to have someone accompany you home tonight."

"Okay." There was something tentative about her voice, like she was trying to hide disappointment. "I'll see you later."

"See you soon." He ended the call.

Evening breezes brushed the trees beyond the perimeter fence. The memory of the feel of Maisy in his arms quickened his pulse. He should've never let them get that close. She'd been sad, they'd both been vulnerable and something inside had drawn them together, like two survivors of the same storm. And now she was stuck to the pieces of his broken heart, and the longer it took before they yanked apart and went their separate ways, the harder it would be.

The blow came out of nowhere, striking him on the back of his skull so hard he felt his knees buckle. The ground rushed toward him. Instinctively, he dropped Queenie's leash as he fell, barely managing to curl into a protective front roll as his body tumbled over the pavement. He leaped up and spun back with his hands raised ready to fight.

A panicked yelp filled his ears and his eyes caught a figure in a dark hoodie disappear down the alley, the frightened beagle clutched to their chest.

Someone was kidnapping Queenie.

ELEVEN

The figure darted around the corner as Queenie's panicked howls filled the air.

"Hey! Stop!" Chase ran after them.

There was no way he was going to let anyone get away with hurting his canine partner. He sprinted around the corner into a side alley, just in time to hear a yelp of pain and a car door slam. A hooded figure in a baseball cap leaped in the door of a small compact car. Queenie's frantic barks sounded from inside the vehicle. The small dog clawed at the passenger window. Chase's heart pounded.

No! The single thought beat through his chest, spurring his legs to move faster. They were not going to hurt Queenie. The vehicle sped down the alley with Queenie inside, howling and yelping for his help. Whoever they were, whatever they wanted, they were not going to get his dog. She was his partner. He was going to protect her with his life. The vehicle darted right and through the empty backstreets, racing down Canyon's back road. His feet pounded down the pavement. The driver swerved wildly, fighting to keep the vehicle straight. Seemed Queenie was putting up a fight. He ran after it, pushing his body past the breaking point, even as he knew he'd never catch up with the car on foot. Where could they go? Where could they hide? The vehicle turned sharply, and suddenly he realized they were making a run for the back perimeter fence. The fastest route there mapped in his mind. The vehicle would have to slow around cement barriers and speed bumps before it reached the perimeter. If he stayed on foot, he could cut them off. He was going to save his dog. He was going to stop this vehicle. He ducked through a back alley, zigzagging through an empty cut through, then he hopped over a short wall and sprinted for the fence.

He stopped, panting and looking down the empty road ahead. The vehicle was nowhere to be seen. He'd been wrong. He'd lost the car and Queenie along with it. He groaned, agony filling his prayer. *Help me, Lord, what do I do? How do I find her?*

A vehicle shot around the corner. A dark hood masked the figure's face. Queenie howled furiously and victoriously, as if she knew Chase was ahead, waiting for her. Without any further thought to his own safety, he leaped in front of the car. The driver hit the brakes. The vehicle spun as tires screeched.

The car crashed through the perimeter fence, rolling and tumbling as it fell down the incline into the ravine forest below, landing in a pond.

Chase's feet stumbled to a stop. The empty hole of the broken fence loomed ahead of him. Justin had warned him the next time he stepped through that fence without permission it could cost him his freedom. But what mattered more? His freedom or his canine partner's life?

He leaped through the fence and scrambled down the hill toward where the vehicle was sinking into the murky water. He kicked off his boots and yanked his phone from his pocket, thankful that Captain Blackwood's number was still near the top of his recent call list.

"Good afternoon, Captain Blackwood—"

"It's Chase," he interrupted. "I'm outside the perimeter fence. Southwest side. Behind the warehouses. Saving my canine partner's life."

He dropped the phone in his boot on the

shore and plunged into the pond. Queenie's panicked howls sounded over the water. She was trapped in the car. It was going under. He splashed through sharp rocks and murky weeds, then he dove under and started swimming hard for the car. Before he could reach it, the door flew open. The hooded figure dove out, their soggy form thrashing furiously against the water as they swam for the far shore. The driver's-side door hung open and water rushed through.

But Queenie didn't follow. Her frantic yelps grew desperate as the car dropped like a stone. The figure was getting away. If he didn't stop them now, he might never know why they were terrorizing him. He might never be able to clear his name or get his life back.

But if he went after them, Queenie would drown.

There was no choice. He had to save his partner. He dove under, his powerful limbs propelling him toward the car. He grabbed the doorway and pushed himself inside, even as he felt it drop deeper underwater. Queenie swam herself into his arms, her paws scrambling against his biceps. He ran his hand along her harness and realized why she couldn't swim. She'd been left there buckled into the seat belt. The injustice and cruelty of that swept through his chest like adrenaline. He fumbled for her lead, unclipped her and then pushed her past him, sending her body up toward the surface. He swam upward, as the car disappeared beneath him, and surfaced beside Queenie. The hooded figure was scrambling away deeper into the ravine, until they disappeared from view. Queenie licked his face furiously as he swam alongside her to shore.

"It's okay," he said. "You're a good dog. You're such a good dog. I've got you now."

But the criminal who'd kidnapped her and terrorized his life was getting away, and with them the last hope he had to save his life and clear his name.

"The little black cat likes milk too," Allie said, guiding the plastic animal into the blockhouse she and Maisy had built on the Sunny Seeds play table. So far, five people and sixteen animals had gathered around the sprawling meal that Allie had concocted. Maisy knelt beside her on the carpet, pulled figures and plastic food from the bins and set them on the table, as Allie seriously considered each one in turn. "White bear likes cookies. Baby wants cupcakes."

Maisy's eyes rose to the clock. It had been half an hour since she'd heard from Chase. Allie had woken up with that kind of boundless, happy energy that only little children seemed to have, and Maisy had found herself needing to fight hard to keep at bay the tears that had been pricking at her eyes. If she hadn't promised Chase that she'd meet him here, she'd have put her spare car seat in her car and taken Allie home.

She needed to get out of Sunny Seeds. She needed to be somewhere safe, where she belonged. Every inch and corner of the preschool held another reminder of the faceless mob in the anonymous blogger's comment section, demanding she lose her job. She'd read the blog again, including all 213 comments. The level of gossip that people were willing to spread about a total stranger was so hateful and vicious it broke her heart. It wasn't just herself, but first Zoe and then Chase, who had also been tried and sentenced by social media. Knowing that made the pain in her heart burn with such a righteous anger that when he'd told her there might be reporters outside her home, she'd wanted to rush home with her head held high and confront them.

Clint Lockwood's daughter never backed

down from a fight. Now, here she was feeling trapped in the one place she didn't want to be, waiting on a man. It was an uncomfortable feeling. But something about Allie's voice, happily chirping beside her as she set up her imaginary party, helped her hold it together.

"How about the airman?" Maisy asked, holding up a figure in camouflage. Normally, the military figures were the most popular toys in the classroom and she practically spent all day refereeing how they were shared. She had to admit there was something fun about having the classroom all to themselves. "Do you think he'd like to sit next to the firefighter or the bunny?"

Allie wrinkled her nose. "No! He's a bad man."

"Members of the United States military are our heroes. It's their job to protect us and keep us safe." The reassuring words flew automatically from Maisy's lips. It wasn't the first time one of her students had reacted badly to a toy or a picture of someone in uniform, just like a student occasionally was afraid of things like dogs, snakes, cars or water. Her instinct was always to defuse the moment lovingly and with logic. "Airmen look out for us and protect us. They're good men and women, like your daddy."

"No! That man is a bad man!" Allie yelled the words with such force it rocked Maisy back on her heels. Her little hand rose in the air as if trying to swat it from Maisy's fingers. "He is a very bad man! Bad man hurt man!"

Something about the toy airman clearly terrified her. Once again FBI special agent Oliver Davison's words that Boyd Sullivan had stolen Drew Golosky's uniform and identification flickered at the back of her mind, sending fresh doubts creeping up Maisy's spine. She only had Chase's word that Allie had been having nightmares about the "bad man" for months, and her terror was so strong and so visceral Maisy would've almost thought Allie had witnessed a crime with her own two eyes.

Was it possible, somehow, that Boyd Sullivan had actually been in Allie's home?

Her cell phone began to ring and Maisy quickly slid the airman figurine under the table and grabbed her phone. It was Chase on the caller ID.

"It's okay, sweetie," Maisy said gently. "We don't have to invite the airman to the party. I need to go talk on the phone for a minute. But I'll stay right in the doorway where you can see me, okay?"

"Okay." Allie's eyes met hers. She picked

a small brown-and-white plastic dog up off the table. "I'm gonna play Doggy, Doggy!"

Maisy smiled. "How about you hide and I'll seek you, after I take this quick phone call?"

"Okay!" Allie smiled. She stood up. Then she waved at her with both hands. "Go! I hide with Doggy now!"

"Okay." She pretended not to notice as Allie dove under the clothing rack. Then she pushed the back door open and felt the delicious warmth of a late summer's afternoon on her limbs.

"Hey, Chase," she said as she answered the call. She braced her body against the door frame, leaving the door open, and pretending not to watch as Allie scampered from one hiding spot to another. "Your daughter just had a really bad reaction to an airman toy. She kept calling him a 'bad man.'"

Chase sighed deeply. "I wish I knew what any of that meant."

"I'm sure you'll figure it out," she said. She closed her eyes and listened to the trees dancing in the summer's breeze on one side and Allie's happy chirps on the other. "I can try to talk to her about it again. I've gotten really good at speaking kid."

"Thank you," he said. She could almost

hear his weariness through the phone. "I'm only about a few minutes away right now, but I wanted to talk to you quickly before I get there. I ran into some trouble."

"What kind of trouble?" She heard sirens then, both in the phone and in the evening air around her. "What's going on? What happened?"

The sirens grew louder. She heard a rustle from behind her in the classroom and a giggle as Allie ran across the room and hid under the table.

"After I left the K-9 training center I decided to walk back to avoid the press," he said. "I stopped in at the warehouse where I used to work in the hopes of talking to my old boss. I was standing in a back alley when someone nearly knocked me down and then stole Queenie."

A gasp rose to Maisy's lips. "Oh, Chase…"

"It's okay," he said quickly. "I ran them down. They crashed through the fence and into a pond. I dove in after her. The figure got away. But Queenie's safe and squirming in my arms now."

Relief filled her chest. *Thank You, God.*

"This has to stop," Chase said. "My daughter, my canine partner, my career, my reputation, you…everything I care about has come under fire. One way or another, I have to stop this."

Two gloved hands clamped around Maisy's throat, throwing her hard against the door frame and knocking the phone from her hands as they stole the air from her lungs. A boot kicked the phone across the yard, cracking the screen and silencing Chase's voice. A hand clamped around her throat, strangling the air from her lungs.

"Get inside," a voice hissed in her ear as the hooded figure tried to shove her through the open door and into the Sunny Seeds classroom. The smell of damp fabric filled her senses. "Give me the girl and I'll let you live."

No! She would not let this criminal get anywhere near Allie.

Maisy kicked up hard, bracing one foot against the door frame as she kicked the door closed with all her might. *Please, Lord, make Chase call the police. Please keep Allie safe until they get here.* Maisy thrashed, trying to wrench herself free. Her attacker hit her, cuffing her on the side of the head. Pain shot through her skull. Bright points of light filled her view. She fell, landing on her hands and knees on the pavement. The figure stood, tall and slender in a plain black hoodie, and reached for the Sunny Seeds classroom door. One gloved hand turned the handle.

No! I can't let them hurt Allie! Please, Lord, please give me the strength I need to save her.

Desperately, Maisy lunged at the figure's knees, hoping to knock them off their feet. But her attacker spun back, shoving Maisy to the ground. She fell and tried to scream, but the figure jumped on her, choking the air from her lungs. Maisy grabbed the attacker's hands, fighting for her life against the stranglehold.

But she was too weak. Pain filled her lungs as prayers filled her mind, even as she felt the darkness sweep over and take hold.

There was nobody there. Nobody to help her. Nobody to save her.

Chase, I'm so sorry, I wasn't strong enough to protect Allie.

TWELVE

She felt her body go limp. The gloved hands fell from her throat and the attacker's weight left her body. She fell to the ground. Moments passed in a haze of darkness and pain before she heard the rattling and crash of her attacker trying to break into the classroom. How long would the door hold? How long until rescue came? Dizziness dragged her mind down into unconsciousness. She battled against it, fighting desperately to stay awake.

Then a shout filtered through the darkness in Maisy's mind. Somewhere on the edges of her unconsciousness she could hear a voice calling her name, strong and powerful, like a beacon, calling to her not to give up hope.

Chase...

A dog was howling, like the hound leading a brigade into battle. *Queenie!* She heard her attacker's footsteps scramble away and a second set of footsteps, larger, stronger and more powerful than her attacker's, pounding hard up the grassy slope and the sound of someone leaping clear over the playground fence.

Then she felt Chase by her side, cradling her, holding her and pulling her into his arms. His hands stroked her hair. His fingers ran along the side of her face and down her bruised throat. She opened her eyes and looked into Chase's deep green gaze.

"Maisy. Baby." His voice was husky, as if he was battling a deeper emotion than his lungs and voice knew how to handle. "What happened? Are you okay? Where's Allie?"

"She's inside." She pointed weakly to the closed door. "Hiding. Safe."

Weakly, she reached past him and punched a security code into the keypad by the door. His lips brushed her forehead, as at the same time he pushed open the Sunny Seeds door. "Allie? Sweet Pea?"

"Daddy!" Allie ran toward them, the relieved smile on her lips battling the worry that filled her eyes. "I was hiding! Maisy didn't find me. Then the door closed with a really loud bang." She stopped and looked down. Her nose crinkled. She reached out and stroked Maisy's head. "You hurt, Maisy?"

"A little bit hurt, sweetie," Maisy said. She

sat up. Chase took her hand and helped her to her feet. "But I'm okay."

She pulled her hand from Chase's fingers, but her legs wobbled so much she almost fell, and she felt Chase tighten his grip on her hand again. Allie grabbed her other hand and squeezed it so tightly, Maisy suspected she was holding it with all her might. Queenie pressed herself against Maisy's calf, in between her and Allie. Maisy stood there for a long moment, drinking in all their care and support, until she felt her head clear and her legs grow steady beneath her.

Then came the clatter of feet. She looked up as Security Forces charged around the corner of the school.

"Chase McLear!" Captain Blackwood called. Maisy watched as his hand twitched over the gun at his side, waiting to see if he needed to pull the trigger. "Kindly step away from the ladies. You and I need to talk."

She felt Chase's hand pull from hers and, instinctively, she swept Allie up into her arms and held her as Chase saluted. "Sir."

"You ran away from the scene of an accident, Airman," Justin said.

"Yes, sir, I did and I'm really glad you all ran after me. Maisy was in trouble. Thankfully, I was there to assist her in time."

Justin's eyes flicked to her face.

"Yes, Justin, he's telling the truth," she said, crossing her arms. "I was attacked. Someone tried to abduct Allie and when I fought them off, they almost strangled me. This is the second kidnap attempt Allie has survived—three, if you count the person we saw lurking in her bushes with a knife. She's been babbling on about a 'bad man' and a 'hurt man.' This child clearly knows something." She stepped forward. "You are my friend, Justin. I respect you deeply as a cop. I have always trusted your investigation into the Red Rose Killer without question. I always believed you would catch him in the end. But now I don't know what to think anymore."

The captain's eyes met hers, strong and unflinching, but nothing in their depths did anything to dispel the questions in her heart.

"Trust me, Maisy," Justin said. "We are pursuing every lead to the utmost of our abilities and capacities."

No, that was not the reassurance she sought. She wanted him to tell her that Chase wasn't a suspect. She wanted him to tell her what Allie was so afraid of and that nobody would hurt that precious child ever again.

"Now," Justin said, his gaze cutting to

Chase's face, "I need to ask you to come with me for questioning. Do you need a few minutes to sort out what you're going to do with your daughter?"

"I'll take her to Zoe and Linc's house," Maisy said. "It's only a few blocks away. Freddy will be happy to see her, and we'll be safe there."

"Thank you," he said softly, his eyes conveying more than his words. He glanced at Justin. "Give me a moment?"

The captain nodded and took a step back. Chase slid his arm around Allie, hugging her with one arm, while the other hand brushed Maisy's shoulder. He leaned forward.

"When I'm done with Captain Blackwood, I'm taking Queenie and going back to the warehouse. I'm going to give her another opportunity to find that scent. I have a former colleague, named Captain Reardon, who knows the facilities even better than I do. I'll see if I can get her to meet me there." Then he pulled back. The look on his face felt somehow more intimate than the kiss they'd shared only a few hours before. "Be careful."

"You too."

"I will be." He took a deep breath and stepped back. "There's something else I need to tell you. I really appreciate you watching

Allie tonight, but that's going to be the last time I ask you to watch her. I'm going to ask for authorization to move off base, and go home to my mother's until this investigation is done. I think it'll be better for Allie, and the cops can put me under surveillance there just as well as they can here. It'll dispel any worries that I'm helping Boyd Sullivan sneak on and off base, and it will relieve the pressure on you. No matter how this ends up, whether I'm charged, discharged or cleared, I'm going to request a transfer to another base. I just don't see a future for myself here. Not anymore. Not after this."

What was he saying? That he and the little girl she held in her arms were leaving her life forever? He kissed his daughter gently on the top of the head, turned and started across the playground toward Captain Blackwood.

Chase felt his shoulders straighten as he walked through the playground and across the parking lot, with Justin on one side and Queenie on the other. He didn't dare let himself turn back. The look in Maisy's eyes had tugged at something deep inside. He hated walking away from her. He hated losing the fledgling relationship they had just started to build. He didn't know what word to put to it.

It went deeper than friendship, deeper than caring or than affection. But whatever it was clung to him, and wrapped around him like roots to a deeply planted tree. It pulled him to her and pulled her to him like an inexorable force. Whatever it was, he'd been denying the existence of it for a long, long time. In fact, he felt like he'd been denying it since the moment he'd first laid eyes on her.

And now, the only way to protect her was to snuff it out, deny it and pretend it never existed.

It wasn't until he reached Justin's vehicle that he realized the captain's eyes were on him, watching him with that familiar pensive look that Chase still didn't know what to make of.

"You really care about her, don't you?" he asked.

Was he really questioning whether or not Chase loved his daughter? No, that was one line too far. He'd had enough of this. Enough of being questioned, poked, prodded at and turned around again and again, until he didn't know which way was up.

"Sir," Chase said. "As I answer that, may I ask you a personal question?"

Justin blinked as if Chase had caught him

by surprise, but he regained his composure almost immediately. "You may."

"Sir, you and I are both fathers," Chase said. His grandfather had taught him a wise man controlled his emotions and Maisy had reminded him that a good man let them flow. Well, maybe he could do both and direct the feelings filling his heart to show this captain once and for all the kind of man he was. "Yes, of course I care about my daughter. I love Allie with my life. I'm all she has after her mother left. I would never do anything to hurt her or put her in harm's way. I have been praying harder than you'll ever know that you'll realize the truth of that and turn your investigation to finding Boyd Sullivan's real accomplice. But for now, with all due respect, Captain, as a man and a father, with a daughter who you love, is there anything in the world that would tempt you to let a violent, controlling and self-entitled killer like Boyd Sullivan into her life?"

A long-drawn-out silence crackled between them. The intensity with which the captain stared at him and sized him up was so relentless Chase guessed it would make a weaker man crumble. Finally, Justin said, "No, Airman, I wouldn't let anyone or anything hurt my daughter, especially not a monster like Sullivan."

He'd hit on something that mattered to the captain and it showed.

"But I wasn't referring to your daughter," Justin added. His shoulders straightened again and the momentary blink of emotion Chase had seen disappeared from his eyes. "I was referring to Maisy Lockwood. Since we're talking personally, I've known Maisy for a very long time. I've never known her to be easily swayed or quick to give her affections away. In fact, I've often thought that she was as reserved and stubborn as her father, in her own very different way, and it would take a man quite a lot to make an impact."

Heat rose to the back of Chase's neck. "I'm sure it's just that she thinks I'm innocent and wants her father's killer caught, sir."

Justin crossed his arms. "Then you're not as smart as I thought you were, or you don't really know Maisy Lockwood."

They went to the station, with Queenie in tow, and once again, Preston was in charge of the interrogation. Justin stood impassively by the wall and watched as Preston fired questions at him, slamming the same horrible pictures down on the table, showing him the victims of Boyd Sullivan's crimes, the bodies, the blood, threatening notes and the red roses tucked under their arms. Preston delved into Chase's record as an airman, pulling at every thread of every tour of duty he'd ever been on. Then he went into Chase's personal life, tearing his most valued relationships to shreds one after another, starting with his mother, father and grandfather. He asked why Liz had left him for another man, whether Allie would be better off without him and if Chase was unfit to be anybody's husband or father.

It was the hardest and harshest of the interrogations Chase had withstood. It was like standing with his hands tied as an unrelenting boxer struck and jabbed at him, blow after blow, trying to knock him bloodied to the ground. All the while Chase sat there, head held high, his answers brief and his voice steady, praying with every breath that God would give him the power to withstand the onslaught.

Why didn't Justin step in and stop Preston? Surely, it was unprofessional for Preston to keep hammering him like that? And yet, the captain stood there in the doorway, without reaction, like a referee with his own reason not to stop the fight.

At least he'd been allowed to take Queenie with him to the interrogation room this time. Feeling his canine partner's reassuring warmth curled up by his ankle gave him a strength that he didn't know he had, encouraging him on, even as he knew his days with her were numbered.

He just prayed that when he left Canyon, Westley would help Queenie find the best possible new partner, someone who would respect, protect and value her, every bit as much as he did. She was a good dog who deserved an opportunity to train and serve her country to her highest potential. She didn't deserve to have Chase holding her back.

Finally, Preston ran out of questions and released him. This time Justin didn't bother warning him not to leave base without informing his office and Chase knew he was leaving Canyon one way or another. The investigation would follow him wherever he went. All he had to do was figure out how to say his goodbyes.

The sun had set below the skyline as he finally exited the building, and the depth of color peeking above the very edges of the horizon took his breath away, reminding him of Maisy. He checked his phone when he left the building. She'd texted him twice to say that she and Allie were happily settled at Linc and Zoe's house and had ordered pizza. A third text showed simply a picture of Allie and Freddy with Star. The desire to phone her, just to hear her voice, welled up inside him with an urgency that was almost painful.

Instead, he squared his shoulders and strode through base toward the warehouses. He dialed his former boss. She picked up on the first ring. "Captain Reardon."

"Hello, ma'am," he said. "It's Chase McLear."

She cleared her throat. "Good evening, Airman. I'm afraid it's not a good time to talk. It's been a rather tiring day."

"I know," he said, as quickly as he dared without actually cutting her off. "I dropped by the warehouse earlier, hoping I could talk to you about the email from Captain Dennis and accessing Ajay's video files, but Security Forces were in your office."

"I'm really sorry, Airman," she said. "But I can't help you. I've been questioned three times about my connection to you, as have several members of my team. Multiple reporters have called me. Our entire office and warehouse complex were searched late this afternoon by officers with K-9 dogs..."

The way Queenie had sounded the alarm when he'd been in the warehouse earlier niggled at the back of his mind. At the time, he'd assumed it was because her training was slipping. What if she'd been trying to tell him something? What if she'd actually smelled something she thought was important?

"Did they find anything?" he asked.

"No." She sounded almost startled by the question. "Of course not."

He guessed he shouldn't have been surprised by the answer. It was hard to imagine anyone stashing a body or illegal explosives in the warehouse. Then again, what if they hadn't sent an electronic-sniffer dog like Queenie?

"Anyway, Captain Dennis told me that several of his men in Afghanistan were interrogated over video call today," Captain Reardon continued, "including Airman Frank Golosky, who is currently mourning the loss of his brother." He winced, and she continued, "Both Captain Dennis and I have been warned by investigators that very serious charges are expected to be filed very shortly and that anyone associated with you could be forced to testify or even face charges themselves."

His breath caught like he'd just been punched in the chest. What charges? How soon would he be arrested? This week? Tomorrow?

Anyone associated with you could be forced to testify or even face charges themselves...

Her words echoed in his mind. Was that why Justin had questioned his feelings for Maisy? Because she would be compelled to testify? Because she was at risk of being charged as an accessory after the fact? It was bad enough that Frank Golosky had been put through the wringer within hours of discovering his brother was dead. The idea of Maisy being hurt even further cut somewhere deeper inside him than he'd ever known was possible. He ran his hand over his head and prayed, *Oh, Lord, what have I done?*

"I'm so sorry for how you've all been impacted by this," he said, bracing himself for what he was about to ask. "But I was wondering if I could come in to talk to you in person? I don't know if you'd made any headway in accessing Ajay Joseph's video files, but maybe I could help look over the data you do have. He'd been concerned about some discrepancies in the transfer logs, and while he'd later assured me it was just a mistake on his end, maybe if I looked at those too, I might see something that would help back up my story. Also, my K-9 dog Queenie started howling when I dropped in to see you earlier. I don't know why, but maybe she smelled something…"

His words trailed off. He sounded so ridiculous. He sounded like a desperate man grasping at the flimsiest straws. But what other choice did he have?

There was a pause, much longer than he liked. He gritted his teeth and prayed.

"I'll be leaving my office in the next twenty minutes," Captain Reardon said, "and then I'll be locking the warehouses down until morning. If you're able to get here before I leave, we can talk briefly. But I can't promise you anything."

"I understand!" Fresh hope surged in his heart. "Thank you, ma'am. I'll be there soon."

Thank You, God!

"Come on, Queenie." He looked down at her hopeful and intelligent face. "We're going back to the warehouse."

He ended the call and sent Maisy a quick text, telling her that he was finished with the questioning and heading to the warehouses for a meeting with Captain Reardon. Then he broke into a jog. Man and dog ran together, past personnel and vehicles. He appreciated each breath of fresh air that filled his lungs and each step his foot made onto the pavement as if it could be his last as a free man.

Finally, he reached the warehouse. They stopped outside the cargo bay door. It was open. Queenie whined. He looked down. She sat expectantly at his feet with her head titled to the side and her intelligent brown eyes locked on his face, waiting for his command to search.

There was something in there she wanted them to find. He knew it with absolute certainty.

Captain Reardon wasn't going to be in her office waiting for him indefinitely. He was on thin ice with his former boss as it was. The logical thing to do was to ignore Queenie, go meet with Captain Reardon and then, after they spoke, ask her if it was okay to let Queenie search the expansive warehouse complex before it shut down for the day, and hope and pray she agreed.

And yet, he couldn't shake the feeling that Queenie really had smelled something on their last visit. Something Queenie had thought was urgent. But he hadn't listened to her. He'd been too quick to doubt her and blame himself for the fact that she was sounding off.

He reached down, ran his hand over her soft fur and scratched her behind the ears. She'd been such a good partner. She'd been loyal and patient, quick to listen and learn, and protective of his daughter, Allie. If this really was his last night as a free man, then maybe he should spend it listening to his partner and trying to decipher what Queenie had been trying to tell him.

"Show me, Queenie. Go search."

She howled and dove through the open doorway with that excited yelp that filled his heart with joy and let him know she was on the scent. He followed her as she weaved and darted through the vehicles, equipment and palettes, heading toward the offices. The warehouse was deserted. But a light still shone from Captain Reardon's office window. He couldn't imagine what she could possibly be thinking to hear Queenie's howls echoing through the warehouses or how it would look if she glanced out her office window to see Chase and Queenie running in circles. But if he found what Queenie smelled and if Captain Reardon could help him clear his name…

Queenie rounded a corner. He followed. Then stopped.

A figure in a dark hoodie, bandanna and baseball cap stood in front of him, a gun raised high in their gloved hands. Chase's hands rose. His feet faltered. But it was too late. The figure fired. A sharp piercing pain caught him in the throat. It was a dart.

"Queenie!" His voice choked. "Run! Hide!"

The last thing he remembered before the

tranquilizer swept over his body, engulfing him and pulling him down into unconsciousness, was the sound of his partner's frantic barking.

THIRTEEN

Allie and Freddy knew they were up past their bedtime. Maisy could tell by the little grins they shared back and forth, as they sat on the floor and played with Freddy blocks, figures and vehicles. They had an entire town of characters spread out over the carpet. She didn't know how late Chase would be. He wasn't answering his phone and Zoe had agreed one late night wouldn't hurt the kids too much.

So instead, she sat in an armchair, her feet curled up beside her and a cup of hot cocoa with marshmallows in her hand, and watched them play. Zoe was on the other side of the room, half lying on the couch, reading something on her laptop. A comfortable quiet spread between them, the kind that said conversation was always available but not needed. Maisy deeply appreciated it.

Her phone buzzed. Her heart leaped and she

snapped it to her ear, thankful it still worked even though the screen was so cracked she could barely see who was calling. “Hello? Chase?”

“It’s Preston,” the caller said stiffly. “I was calling to ask if you could meet me at the Winged Java for a late coffee tonight. I have some news I want to share with you in person.”

A late-night coffee date with Preston? She was sure that Zoe would be more than happy to watch Allie for a little bit if she asked, and with Linc and Star home too she had no doubt Allie would be safe. But did she really want to meet Preston for a late-night anything? She took a deep breath. “No, Preston. I won’t meet up with you outside of work or professional duties. If there’s anything you need to tell me, it can wait until morning.”

“I’m calling to inform you that a warrant is being issued as we speak for Chase McLear’s arrest,” he blurted so quickly his voice was almost petulant. “It’s the end of the line for him. He’s going to be kicked out of the canine program—which is about time, considering some of us have been waiting a whole lot longer than he did to get partnered with a dog. He’s going to spend the rest of his life in jail.”

“A warrant? For what?” She stood. Zoe’s

eyes met hers. Maisy mouthed the word *Preston*. Then she stepped across the room to the window. "What are you talking about?"

"New irrefutable evidence has come to light that proves Chase McLear has been helping Boyd Sullivan," Preston said. "Photos turned up on a security camera that showed him talking with Boyd Sullivan and Drew Golosky at a gas station near the ravine. What's worse is his daughter was in the back of his truck, watching the whole thing."

"That can't be possible," she said. Yet, it fit all the facts of the case as she knew it, from why Allie was babbling about a "bad man," to why someone had reported seeing Boyd Sullivan at Chase's home, to why Boyd, or another accomplice, might try to kidnap Allie.

But it didn't match the heart of the man she saw in Chase's eyes.

"Well, it's true," Preston said. He sounded disappointed. Sulky, even. Like a child who was watching his balloon float away or who had dropped his ice-cream cone on the ground. No, more like a preschool child who'd suddenly decided he wanted the toy some other child was playing with to be his. "I thought you'd be happy that I caught Boyd Sullivan's accomplice! I did it! Me! Because I knew he was guilty all along. I knew it when he was chosen to work with that electronic-sniffing dog over me. I knew it when I asked Yvette if you were seeing anyone, weeks ago, and she told me she thought you had a crush on him. You never saw him for what he was. Nobody did anything to stop him. Nobody tried to protect you from him. So I stepped up and made it happen."

"Made it happen?" she said. "How? That's not how this works, Preston. You don't suspect someone's guilty and prove it. You follow the evidence."

"Trust me. The evidence will prove he's guilty!"

Foreboding filled her heart. What had Preston done?

"Bad man!" Allie yelped, pushing away the toy that Freddy was trying to put in his small parade of figures. "Bad man, no!"

What did that mean? Why did it matter so much to Allie that her chin was quivering?

"No!" Freddy said. "He's good man! Like my new daddy, Linc!"

"I'm sorry, Preston," Maisy said. "I don't want to talk to you any further about this. I'll get my updates on the case from Captain Blackwood. I've got to go."

He was still sputtering as she hung up. She dropped down on her knees beside the children on the carpet and gently pulled the toy airman from where it was trapped between Allie's and Freddy's hands.

"Why is this a bad man, Allie?" Maisy asked gently.

Allie's eyes welled with tears.

Help me, Lord. I can't save Chase. I can't find Boyd Sullivan, the lost dogs or stop false charges from being laid. But with Your help, maybe I can break through to this frightened little girl's heart.

"Let's tell a story about the bad man, okay, Allie?" she asked, keeping her voice cheerful and upbeat, in her usual teacher storytelling voice. "We can work together to tell the story about the bad man, okay? It'll be safe, because we'll be in charge of how the story goes, okay?"

Allie paused for a long moment. Maisy's heart ached and prayed. Then Allie nodded. "Bad man hurt man."

Oh, honey, I know that means so very much to you. Help me understand and why it makes you shake and cry.

"Well, then," Maisy said, "we need to find somebody to play the hurt man." She picked another airman from the pile of toys. "How about him? Can he be the hurt man?"

Allie shook her head. "No."

"Okay, how about the pilot?"

"No." Her tiny forehead wrinkled and then she turned and searched through the toys with the kind of meticulous care that took forever. Finally, she pulled out a bearded shepherd that Maisy guessed was from a nativity set.

"This!" she said proudly. "This is hurt man!"

Allie took the "bad man" from Maisy's hand, looked around for a moment and then ran over to Zoe's laptop. She made the tiny figure of the "hurt man" jump up and down in front of Zoe's laptop screen. Then bringing her small hands together quickly, the "bad man" hit the "hurt man" with a force so loudly the sound of plastic against plastic seemed to shake the room. The "hurt man" fell onto the floor.

Zoe's eyes met Maisy's, filled with worry.

"Is this something you saw on the television?" Zoe asked softly.

Allie shook her head. "On Daddy's com puter."

"Was your daddy there when you watched it?" Maisy asked.

Allie shook her head. "Hurt man said, 'Hi, I'm Daddy's friend. Who are you?' And I said, 'Allie.' And he said, 'I'm…'"

Her forehead crinkled. Maisy's heart shuddered.

"Was it Drew?" Zoe asked. Allie shook

her head. "Was it Boyd?" Allie shook her head again.

Maisy took in a breath and guessed. "Was it Ajay?"

Tears filled Allie's eyes. Maisy clutched her to her chest and held her tightly.

"You did a very good job telling your story, Allie. You're a very brave girl." She looked up and met Zoe's gaze over Allie's head. "Ajay is an Afghan local and Chase's alibi for the morning that Boyd broke onto base. I need to talk to Chase. He's been trying to reach him for weeks. And if Allie's story is true..."

Her voice trailed off. Zoe nodded slowly. She knew without Maisy saying the words. Then Chase's alibi had been dead for months and Allie had witnessed the murder.

"I think it's time to make s'mores," Zoe said brightly. "I think Linc would like to help us make a fire. Would you like that, Allie?"

"S'mores!" Freddy jumped to his feet.

Allie nodded. "I like marshmallows."

"So do I," Zoe said. She set her laptop down and reached for Allie with one hand and Freddy with another. Then she glanced at Maisy. "I'll be in either the kitchen or the backyard if you need me."

Zoe led the two children into the kitchen. Maisy dialed Chase's number. It rang. What did it mean that the man who Chase considered his alibi had been killed? Would it make any difference to the fact that Chase was going to be arrested tonight?

The phone call went through to his voice mail. She tried again and got voice mail a second time. Did that mean he'd already been arrested? Or did he have his phone off while he was meeting with Captain Reardon?

Help me, Lord, what do I do? If Preston's right, Chase is going to be arrested tonight. But if this is one piece of evidence that could help him or save him in any way...

She opened her eyes, grabbed her purse and her keys. The warehouse complex was less than a ten-minute drive away. She could get there, tell Chase and be back before the s'mores were even finished. If all went well, she'd catch him before he was arrested.

"I'll be back soon," she called. "I'm just going to go talk to Chase."

She ran for the door. Nine minutes later, she'd reached the warehouse. The door was open. The warehouse was dark. She pulled her phone out and turned on the flashlight.

"Chase?" She stepped in. Darkness and shadows of vehicles and palettes of equipment loomed around her. Her footsteps echoed in the darkness. "Chase? Are you in here?"

Nothing but silence filled her ears.

Where had he gone? Was she too late?

Then she heard a faint sound of whimpering. She ran toward it. "Queenie!"

The whimpering turned into a howl, then she felt a small furry body launch itself against her. Maisy dropped to her knees, brushed her hand over the small dog's soft fur and felt the gentle tip of Queenie's tongue touch her fingers. "Queenie, where's Chase? Find Chase."

Darkness filled Chase's gaze. He tried to move, but he seemed to be wedged sideways in something very dark with his long limbs cramped around him. He groaned. Cloth filled his mouth. He'd been gagged, his hands were tied behind his back and his legs were bent beneath him at an odd angle. The tranquilizer was wearing off slowly, leaving behind a horrible grogginess that filled his mouth with a vile taste and made his limbs feel like wet cement. He tried to sit up and smacked his head on something metal.

He was in the trunk of a car, a small one by the feel of it. He felt around. No tools. No latch he could easily access, either. But at least the vehicle didn't seem to be moving. Not for now, anyway.

He closed his eyes and prayed. *God, I need Your help.* All this time he'd felt like he was just one step ahead of the people who wanted to lock him away. Now he was well and truly trapped.

The idea of Allie growing up without him hurt so deeply he couldn't breathe. Then Maisy's face filled his mind. Why hadn't he told her how he felt? Even if she'd rejected him, she still deserved to know that in his eyes she was extraordinary and that if he could, he'd spend every last day of this life letting her know how special she was.

Then he heard a stubborn and determined howl and it filled his chest with hope. Queenie had found him.

"This way? Is this where he is? Chase? Chase can you hear me?" Then he heard a voice that made his heart beat even faster. The one voice his poor feeble heart would know anywhere. It was Maisy and she was looking for him.

"Maisy!" he shouted as loudly as he could, forcing his voice through the gag. His strong legs kicked hard against the trunk. *"Maisy! I'm in here!"*

"Chase!" Her fists rapped against the trunk. "Hang on, Chase, I'm coming!" He heard her hands struggle with the latch. Queenie's howls rose. “It’s locked. Hang on. I’m going to open it from the front seat.”

She disappeared for the longest single moment he’d ever experienced in his life. Then he heard the sound of a window smashing. The latch clicked and the trunk opened. He sat up.

He was in the trunk of a small car in a different part of the same warehouse. He guessed he’d surprised whoever had attacked him and they hadn’t had long to plan. The question was where they’d gone now and what they were going to do next.

“I broke the front window,” Maisy said. Her face appeared around the corner, dim in the darkness and lit by her cell phone flashlight, and he knew without a doubt that she was the most beautiful person he’d ever seen in his life. “I can’t tell you how amazing it is to see you!”

Her hands flew around his neck. Her fingers fumbled to loosen the gag. The fabric fell from his mouth. Her face hovered just inches from his. He leaned forward and kissed her, letting his lips brush against hers for just a moment before her hands slid down to his back and untied his hands.

“Thank you,” he breathed.

“No problem,” she said. “I wouldn’t be

much of a preschool teacher if I didn't know how to untie some pretty difficult knots."

He reached for her face. His fingers brushed her cheeks.

"Thank you for coming to find me," he said. "Thank you for believing in me and never giving up on me. I never dreamed I'd have someone as special as you in my life."

Her eyes flickered to his face. Then his lips met hers again, softly and sweetly. He kissed her for one long moment that seemed to contain a lifetime of longing. Then he pulled back, reached down, untied his feet and leaped from the trunk.

"Good dog." He reached down and brushed the top of Queenie's head. Then he grabbed Maisy's hand. "Come on, we need to find Captain Reardon and get out of here."

Through the maze of equipment and palettes he could see a dim light still shining in her office window. It was unimaginable that she hadn't heard Queenie's howls and realized something was wrong. Had she called the police? Had she hidden? Had his attacker gotten to her too?

"Wait." Her fingers tightened in his. "I have things I have to tell you quickly. First, Preston said charges are going to be brought against you tonight. They claim to have pictures of you, Boyd Sullivan, Drew Golosky and Allie together at a gas station."

"They're fake," he said. "That never happened. I wouldn't do that."

He started to pull his hand from her grasp, but she held on to him tightly.

"I know, Chase," she said. "I believe you. I know the man you are inside. There's more. I got Allie to tell me who the 'bad man' and the 'hurt man' are. The 'hurt man' is your alibi, Ajay. The 'bad man' is someone who killed him while he was on video chat with your daughter."

His heart stopped. Ajay was dead and his own little girl had witnessed his murder? But who had killed him? And why?

"Down on the ground, both of you, or I'll shoot you."

A hooded figure in a baseball cap and bandanna stepped out of the darkness, and Chase heard for the first time the voice of the person who'd been terrorizing him and realized just who the figure behind the mask was.

FOURTEEN

"Captain Reardon," he called. "It's you, isn't it?"

Chase dropped to the ground, holding one hand above his head and keeping the other clasped tight in Maisy's hand. Now that he found her, he never wanted to let her go.

"You were behind this the whole time, weren't you?" he said. "Don't deny it. I know your voice. What's your game here? Are you working with the person who was stealing the weapons? Did you have something to do with Ajay getting murdered? Are you working with Boyd Sullivan?"

"I have nothing to do with Boyd Sullivan!" The captain tossed her head, letting the hood fall back as she pulled the bandanna from her lips. "He was a convenient way to discredit you. People on this base are all too eager to find someone to fear and hate. This is about a small scale black market weapons business that was going just peachy until Ajay Joseph decided to look too hard at the shipping manifests, and Teddy Dennis was stupid enough to kill him when he tried to video call you about it, not realizing your little brat had witnessed it."

He felt Maisy squeeze his hand. He squeezed hers back tightly.

"So you and Captain Dennis concocted a brilliant plan to steal and sell hundreds of thousands of dollars' worth of weapons from the United States Air Force and kill a good man to make that happen, and my toddler managed to ruin your plan."

Oh, his beautiful little girl was so smart and so brave. She'd been trying to tell him all along. But it took Maisy's kind and patient love to bring it out of her.

"What's your plan here, Captain Reardon?" he asked. "You tried to take my daughter, so she couldn't tell anyone what happened. You tried to take my dog, because you knew she'd tracked something. You tried to kill Maisy for protecting my daughter from you. Why take me? To kill me in some way that framed me and ended this?"

"I didn't work this hard, for this long, to skim just the right amount not to get caught, find buyers, move weapons and coordinate all that, only to have your kid, your little dog and a preschool teacher ruin it for me," Captain Reardon snarled.

A wry smile turned on Chase's lips. His kid, his little dog and a preschool teacher. He couldn't think of a team he'd rather be a part of. He eased his fingers from Maisy's, stood up slowly and took a step forward, putting himself between Captain Reardon's gun and Maisy. As far as he knew, his former captain hadn't actually murdered anyone yet. Each time she'd attacked, she'd hesitated or run. He hoped that meant he could keep her from pulling the trigger now.

"Stop! Right now, Chase! Another step and I'll shoot her through the head!"

Well, that settled it. He threw himself at Captain Reardon, catching her by the wrist, clamping his hands over hers before the gun could fire. She fell backward as he broke her grasp on the gun. Then he stood over her, aiming the weapon at her head.

"Get down! Stay down!" Chase shouted. "This ends here!"

"Yeah it does, Chase!" a man's voice echoed. "But not for her!"

Light filled his eyes. He blinked as a man in a Security Forces uniform strode toward him. It was Preston.

"Get down! On the ground! Drop your weapon!" Preston barked. "This time, I've got you dead to rights! You're going to prison for the rest of your life."

Chase tossed the gun so hard it ricocheted somewhere deep inside the warehouse and knelt. He knew how this looked. Preston had been itching for a reason to throw him in jail for days, and now he had him red-handed, with a weapon pointed at a superior officer and no proof of a reason why.

"Preston, wait!" Maisy darted in front of him, stepping between Preston and Chase. "You've got it all wrong, Preston. Listen to me, please. Captain Reardon framed Chase because one of Chase's old colleagues figured out that she and Captain Dennis were working together to steal from weapon shipments. Her accomplice in Afghanistan killed Chase's alibi, Ajay Joseph. Chase's daughter, Allie, witnessed the murder."

But still, one important question remained unanswered. What had Queenie smelled? How had Captain Reardon possibly gotten her hands on the gold cross and planted it?

"Whatever he says, Lieutenant, don't believe him," Captain Reardon said. She got to her feet. Her eyes scanned in vain for her gun. "Neither of them can prove a word of any of that."

"No," Chase said. "We can't. But I think I know who can." He turned to his little dog, standing obediently for her partner's word, even as he was in danger. "Queenie, search."

She disappeared with a howl, charging through the warehouse with her nose on the scent. Then she barked triumphantly and stood up on her hind legs, with her paws braced against Captain Reardon's office door.

Chase leaped to run after her, but Preston's gun kept him in place.

"She's found something," Chase said. "Let me go see what it is."

"You stay there," Preston said. "I don't care what she's found. If you move, I'll shoot you."

Captain Reardon smirked. Panic beat through Chase's chest. If there was something hiding in Captain Reardon's office and Preston didn't let him search for it, she could destroy it or remove it before anyone could ever find it.

"But you wouldn't shoot me, would you, Preston?" Maisy asked.

Chase wasn't so sure. Was Preston's jealousy so twisted he'd kill Maisy for rejecting him? But Chase could only watch as Maisy broke into a sprint, running through the darkened parking lot toward the small dog.

"Stay out of my office!" Captain Reardon shouted. She ran at Maisy. But it was too late. Maisy yanked the office door open. Queenie darted through, with Maisy on her heels. She slammed the door shut behind her and turned the lock. Captain Reardon pounded her fists on her office door. She glanced at Preston. "Shoot the lock off!"

Preston hesitated. The office blind flew up.

"Chase!" Maisy shouted. Her face appeared at the office window. The glass was so flimsy she barely had to raise her voice to be heard. There was no way it was bulletproof. "Queenie's pawing the carpet!"

"Yank the carpet up and look underneath!" Chase shouted, ignoring the gun barrel aimed at his temple. If Preston flinched, even so much as an inch to turn the gun away from Chase's face and toward Maisy and the office, Chase would be able to use the distraction to catch him by the wrist and force him to the floor.

Maisy disappeared from view.

"There's a floor grate under the carpet!" she shouted. "Hang on."

Her voice disappeared. Captain Reardon's

hand paused on the door as a clammy paleness spread over her face.

Then a happy laugh filled the air.

"Chase!" Maisy's face appeared at the window, holding a blue-cased laptop. "Queenie's found a computer!"

"That's mine, isn't it?" Chase asked his former boss. But even if he hadn't recognized the laptop cover, the panicked look on Captain Reardon's ashen face would've confirmed his suspicion. He glanced at Preston, meeting his eyes over the barrel of the gun. "That's the laptop I told you was stolen from my truck. It'll have proof of my conversations with Ajay, the encrypted files he sent of the weapons transfers, his murder, all of it. Even if Captain Reardon was smart enough to try to wipe it, the machine has a secret backup drive."

Maisy disappeared from the window. Preston hesitated. Fear, anger and frustration filled his eyes. Then Chase realized that Captain Reardon had stopped trying to break into her office. Instead, she stood by the office door with her arms crossed and her lips pursed, as frozen as a computer trying to process new information. He knew that look. She was calculating.

A moment later, Maisy was back at the

window. "I tried to call Justin, but the office phone's dead. I can't get a signal on my cell phone, either."

Help us, Lord. You're our only hope.

"The laptop doesn't matter," Preston said. "We still have the gold cross. Nothing on that machine will clear you of the fact that Maisy's father's cross was found in your home."

"Because you planted it there, didn't you, Preston?" Maisy shouted. "Don't lie to me. I spend all day settling squabbles between little children. You think I can't tell when someone's guilty of something? You told me yourself, you wanted to solve the crime. So what happened? You found my father's cross at a crime scene and decided that rather than processing it properly you'd hold on to it?"

"Because I wanted to give it back to you myself!" Preston roared.

"Because you wanted to be a hero!" Maisy's voice rose. "When Captain Reardon decided to try to frame Chase as Boyd's accomplice, and Security Forces searched Chase's home, you saw your opportunity to kill two birds with one stone. Captain Reardon stumbled into a desperate crime to protect herself. Little did she know she was only getting away with it because you were too focused on proving that Chase was guilty to actually do your job!"

"Because I knew he was guilty!" Preston snapped. "And if I had to plant evidence to make sure he got what was coming to him and he went to prison, it was worth it."

"Enough of this!" Captain Reardon shouted. Whatever she'd been debating in her mind had apparently been decided. "Shoot out the office window. We can make it look like an accident and because it's a big target, it'll look less suspicious than if we break down my office door. I'll go in and drag her out. You take him and we'll kill them both. I'll have your back. Nobody needs to know about any of this. I'll cut you in and I'll make it worth your while. Your problems will go away and so will mine."

Fear filled Chase's veins as he watched Preston hesitate, and Chase could see without a doubt that he was considering it. Maybe he'd been right that Captain Reardon wasn't prepared to commit murder. But the fact that her accomplice, Captain Dennis, had killed Ajay meant that clearly she wasn't above getting somebody else to do her dirty work.

"Let Maisy go!" Chase stepped forward, his hands raised. "Do whatever you want to me, but don't hurt Maisy. Let her go and be there for my daughter."

"Chase, no!" His name flew from Maisy's lips like a cry.

But he raised a hand and signaled her to hold back and trust him.

"You have to kill them both," Captain Reardon said. "It's the only way. We can leave them in the ravine, with a rose and everything, and make it look like Boyd Sullivan killed them."

"Preston," Chase said firmly. "She's guilty of treason and an accomplice to murder. The only thing you're guilty of is planting evidence."

Preston raised his weapon, steadied it with his second hand, and Chase knew without a doubt in his mind that Preston wouldn't miss the shot.

"Think about it, Preston!" Captain Reardon's voice rose. "You're going to walk out of here one of two ways. Either you're going to be seen as a corrupt cop who planted evidence to frame someone. Or everyone will celebrate you as the man who brought down the Red Rose Killer's accomplice! Maisy is Clint Lockwood's daughter. Boyd Sullivan is probably going to kill her eventually, anyway."

"I'm sorry, Maisy, but she's right," Preston said. "You should've let me save you."

"Maisy!" Chase shouted. "Get back!"

Queenie howled. Chase leaped. The weapon fired. The bullet flew. The office window shattered in a spray of glass fragments. Chase threw Preston to the ground, yanking the weapon from his grasp. Preston reared back. His fists flew toward Chase's face. But it was too late. Chase caught him by the arm and flipped him, pressing him face down into the pavement.

"Maisy!" he shouted. His eyes darted toward the empty and gaping hole where the windowpane had been. *Please, Lord, let her be okay.* Preston squirmed beneath him, fighting his hold. Captain Reardon ran for the office window, braced her hand on the window frame and prepared to leap through, destroy the laptop and Maisy. "No!"

Maisy jumped up, her face flushed, her eyes determined and an office chair clutched in her hands. She swung at the captain. His former boss shouted in pain and crumpled to the floor. Emotions surged through his chest in a wave that seemed to crash over him. Relief. Thankfulness. Admiration.

Love.

Footsteps sounded in the distance, then shouting and the sound of dogs barking.

He looked up as a group of well-armed Security Forces swarmed around them, with Captain Justin Blackwood at the lead.

"Justin!" Maisy unlocked the office door, pushed through and ran toward him, clutching the laptop to her chest, with Queenie at her heels. "Stop! Chase is innocent. Preston planted the gold cross. Captain Reardon called in the fake Boyd Sullivan sighting to cover up a murder overseas. This laptop has the proof of Chase's alibi and how he was murdered."

"I heard," Justin said. His mouth set in a grim line. "We had Preston under surveillance."

What? Chase loosened his grip on Preston, but not enough that the man could actually stand.

"You can let him up," Justin said. "We'll take it from here. We had reason to suspect for some time that he'd tampered with some evidence in order to boost his own ego."

Did that mean Chase had been used as bait, in some trap, to allow them to catch Preston? That when Justin had seen how relentlessly Preston had gone after him, he'd stepped back and let Chase withstand his attacks, in order to reach the truth?

Yet, he knew, as he looked at Justin's face, that he'd never get an answer to that question.

Two officers flanked Captain Reardon, even as she groaned and stumbled to her feet.

Justin looked from Chase to Maisy and back again. "What happened to her?"

"I hit her with a chair," Maisy said.

Justin snorted. His deep laugh seemed to rumble through the warehouse. "Well, this afternoon our tech team traced the IP address of the person who'd sent Canyon's anonymous blogger those pictures and story about you to her office computer. Unfortunately, the blogger themself changed servers before we could track them down."

Chase hoped that meant they were one step closer to figuring out who was running the blog and shutting it down.

Justin straightened his uniform.

"Airman Chase McLear, you're free to go," he added. "I'll also be speaking to the K-9 unit shortly and letting them know my recommendation that you and Queenie be reinstated to the K-9 program immediately."

Gratitude bubbled like a fountain inside Chase's heart. But Maisy's arms crossed against her chest.

"Not so fast, what about the pictures of Chase and Allie with Drew Golosky and Boyd Sullivan?" Maisy demanded. "They must be fakes."

"They're very well-made fakes." Justin's mouth twitched slightly and suddenly Chase had a suspicion that someone within the investigation had created them to tip Preston's hand. "But nevertheless fakes, I assure you."

A thousand questions filled Chase's mind that he suspected he'd never get answers to no matter how many times he asked. Instead, he straightened himself up to his full height and saluted. "Thank you, sir."

Justin returned his salute. "Thank you, Airman."

Chase stood back and called Queenie to his side. He watched as Preston and Captain Reardon were arrested, and an officer took the laptop from Maisy. Then he felt Maisy step to his side and her fingers brush his. He took her hand and held it tightly.

"Come on," he said. "Let's go get Allie."

They walked out, hand in hand, with Queenie. He drove back to Linc and Zoe's house in comfortable silence, with one hand on the steering wheel and the other holding Maisy's fingers gently and never wanting to let her go. They found Allie, curled up at one end of the couch, with Freddy on the other end and Star lying on the floor between them. Maisy walked over and quietly filled Zoe in on what had happened and promised to tell her more in the morning.

Chase reached for his daughter. "Hey, Sweet Pea."

"Hi, Daddy." Allie smiled sleepily, raising her hands toward him as he pulled her into his arms. She laid her head on his chest. He ran his hand over her head.

"We found out who the bad man is and how to stop him," he whispered. "We also found the bad lady who grabbed you and that loud rude man from earlier. Some very good men and women are going stop all of them and make sure they never hurt anyone ever again, thanks to you."

"That's good, Daddy." She yawned. Her eyes closed. "Is Maisy here? I made us a new house, with blocks, for you, and me, and Queenie..." She yawned again. "And Maisy, all together."

He looked down. There on the floor was a small house made of wooden blocks. Inside, she'd propped up the figures of an airman and a blonde in a sparkling white dress. The two figures were holding hands. A little blonde girl and a tiny dog stood beside them.

He looked up over the top of his daughter's head. Maisy's beautiful eyes met his.

"Come on," he whispered. They walked outside of the house into the warm Texas night. The sky was a wash of deep blue-black above their heads, dotted with the bright light of what felt like a thousand stars. He slid Allie into her car seat. She'd already fallen back asleep by the time he'd buckled her in. He held the door long enough for Queenie to leap into the back seat after her. She lay down, her small snout resting protectively on Allie's arm.

Chase shut the door quietly. Then he turned to Maisy, reached for both of her hands and held them in his. Her eyes sparkled and the light in them was brighter and more beautiful than every star that spread above them in the sky.

"That was a very pretty house Allie built for us," he said softly. "It's a bit too small for us. But I liked her idea of us all being a family together."

She stepped toward him. "I do too."

He took both her hands in his and pulled her in closer to him.

"Captain Reardon was right about one thing. You might be a target of Boyd Sullivan's. I'd feel better knowing I was there keeping you safe. Plus, Allie loves you so much." He took a deep breath and felt the words he'd been dying to say for longer than he could remember. "And I'm in love with you, Maisy. I love your eyes and your smile. I love the way you think and the way you care for others. I love you in a way that I never knew it was possible to love. And I'm hoping very much you'll consider marrying me and becoming my wife, Allie's mother and a member of our family." The smile that lit up her eyes was all the answer he needed. But still, he couldn't wait to hear her say the words. He pulled her closer. "You're something special, Maisy. I'm sorry if this seems sudden, but I feel like I've been waiting to say these words ever since the day we met."

"I feel the same way about you," Maisy said as she ran her hands up around his neck. He slid his arms around her waist. "I love you, Chase, and yes, I would really love to marry you and be Allie's mother."

He lifted her up into his arms and his lips met hers in a kiss for one long and beautiful moment, as a greater happiness than he ever expected to feel filled his heart. Then he set her back down and held her to his chest, as he raised his eyes to the sky and whispered a prayer of thanks, under a canopy of dazzling Texas stars.

* * * * *

The hunt for the Red Rose Killer continues.
Look for the next exciting stories in the
MILITARY K-9 UNIT *series:*

MISSION TO PROTECT—Terri Reed,
April 2018
BOUND BY DUTY—Valerie Hansen,
May 2018
TOP SECRET TARGET—Dana Mentink,
June 2018
STANDING FAST—Maggie K. Black,
July 2018
RESCUE OPERATION—Lenora Worth,
August 2018
EXPLOSIVE FORCE—Lynette Eason,
September 2018
BATTLE TESTED—Laura Scott,
October 2018
VALIANT DEFENDER—Shirlee McCoy,
November 2018
MILITARY K-9 UNIT CHRISTMAS—
Valerie Hansen and Laura Scott,
December 2018

Dear Reader,

Have you ever felt like an outsider or been outside a group looking in? Eight years ago, I stood in a hotel lobby at the American Christian Fiction Writers Conference, trying to get up the nerve to go talk to a group of Love Inspired authors. There they were, sitting in a line under the escalator, typing away and talking about poison. I summoned my courage and admitted I wanted to write books like theirs. Lynette Eason invited me to sit with them and ask questions.

That day my life changed. I met my wonderful editor, Emily Rodmell, who edited this Military K-9 Unit series, that afternoon. A year later, I submitted a book, and while it wasn't accepted, Emily provided me with helpful notes and Lynette encouraged me to try again. I did and one year later, Emily called to tell me Love Inspired would be publishing *Killer Assignment*.

Being part of this K-9 series, which includes books by some of my own writing heroines, is a dream come true. I really identified with Chase and Maisy, who both felt like outsiders, and I loved watching their romance unfold. I hope you enjoyed it too.

If you want to find out more about writing for Love Inspired, visit www.soyouthinkyoucanwrite.com, follow Emily on Twitter at @EmilyRodmell or find her on Facebook at 'Emily Rodmell, Editor' for tips and advice. You can find me on Twitter at @MaggieKBlack or at www.maggiekblack.com.

Thank you for sharing this journey with me.

Maggie